LOVE'S CONFLICT • FLORENCE MARRYAT

General Books LLC™, Memphis, USA, 2012. ISBN: 9780217859554.

❖ ❖ ❖ ❖ ❖ ❖ ❖ ❖

LOVE'S CONFLICT. CHAPTER I. PAST AND GONE.

Grace was by her bedside, but Elfrida was too ill to derive much comfort from her presence. The brother adviser had arrived, and was sitting with Dr. Henderson and William Treherne in the lower room, where they were all three making themselves very comfortable, and whence the medical gentlemen occasionally issued to take their way with stealthy steps to the sick room. Grace's sad and anxious eyes raised to theirs could gain little of their opinion of her sister's case from their expression, but her heart told her that all was not right, as she sat hour after hour by the bedside, and heard the frag/i-mentary, rambling talk, only stifled by her heavy moans. However, this could not go on for ever. As VOL. III. B the night wore on, the doctors had another consultation, and then Grace was shut out of the room, and told to go down stairs and wait. A weary time, during which she listened, with the beatings of her heart nearly stopped, to every footstep on the stairs, in hopes it might come towards the drawing-room, and bring her news. A time during which she could only put up prayers for her sister's safety, and wait tremblingly for the result.

But it came at last. As the dull November morning broke, and the light commencing to peer through the shutter chinks, made Grace begin to think of putting out her candles and letting in the daylight, the handle of the door turned. She had watched for it so long and wearily, that now it came, it almost took her by surprise.

"Ellen!" she exclaimed, as the house-maid came in, with a face full of bustling importance, "is it

"Lor—yes, miss—half an hour ago; a little boy; and the doctor wants to speak with you in mistress's dressing-room."

With a " Thank God" upon her lips, Grace waited to hear no more; but running up-stairs as noiselessly as she could, sought the dressing-room at once. It was a very handsome room for that designation, being large, and amply furnished with all the luxuries that the mysteries of female dressing require. At the present time it seemed full of people, all earnest and busy; and directly Grace entered, she saw that something had gone wrong. Dr. Henderson and his professional friend were standing in close consultation with William Treherne, whilst Mrs. Meade, the all-important nurse, sat close to the blazing fire, regally ensconced in a luxurious arm-chair, with a bundle of flannel on her lap; but there was a gravity —not to say pity—engraved on all their faces, which made Grace start forward as she saw it, exclaiming— pings of flannel, which Mrs. Meade only seemed to draw still closer.

"Oh, sir! there is nothing wrong with my sister, is there T

It was Dr. Henderson she had addressed, and the look he turned upon her was perfectly reassuring.

"No, my dear young lady, I trust not. Mrs. William Treherne is doing very nicely; but I am afraid we shall not save the infant."

Then all Grace's womanly feelings were turned into that direction, as were her eyes.

"Oh, why not? poor little darling. Nurse, let me see it." And she tried to pull away the wrap

"You'd better not look at it, miss," was her pitying answer; "'tisn't a sight for such as you."

"What is the matter?" said Grace, thoroughly alarmed.

"Nonsense, Mrs. Meade," said the doctor; " shew the infant to Miss Salisbury. I particularly wish her to see it. The fact is, my dear young lady, it's a sad case. The child has evidently received some injury previous to birth, and the vital ebb is low— very low indeed. We wished to see you about breaking the news to Mrs. Treherne. Mrs. Meade, uncover the child."

Then the monthly nurse, with a

strange look in her face—quite unlike her usual professional pride i when she first honoured visitors with the sight of a new-comer—laid back the folds of flannel, and showed Grace the new-born child. Not unlike other new-born children in the little inexpressive, highlycoloured face, but very unlike in the tender limbs, bent and twisted by some cruel accident of mind or body, in the curved spine, the injured chest, the quick, hard breathing, which told that the tiny lungs were unable to perform their work, and would cease the painful task before long. As Grace looked at the poor little deformed creature, just lying placidly and breathing its brief life away, the tears welled up beneath her eyelids, and dropped silently upon the tender naked limbs and nurse's hard-worn hands.

"Don't take on, miss," was that worthy's whispered comfort; "it don't suffer, pretty dear, and it 'll soon be gone and at rest."

But the woman's own eyes filled as she quietly covered up the little body again, which it had not been thought worth while to dress.

"May I ask," said the mild voice of Dr. Henderson to William Treherne, "if your lady has experienced any shock during the last few months—any serious shock, either of mind or body *T*

This question made Grace turn her attention to her brother-in-law. William Treherne did not appear very much grieved at the idea of losing his first-born. Indeed, he was relieved than otherwise, as the child was deformed, on hearing that it was impossible it could live.

To Dr. Henderson's question he now gave a decided "No I"

"There has been no cause of grief, no mental strain?" urged the doctor.

"No, not that I know of."

"Oh, William," urged Grace, "you forget poor mamma!"

Mr. Treherne then intimated that his wife had lost her mother a few months previously.

"Unexpectedly?—was the shock very great? I can see, Mr. Treherne," added Dr. Henderson, "that your lady is of a very excitable and highly nervous temperament. The fainting fits to which she has been subject are attributable to the same cause. Some circumstance or thing has worked very powerfully, however, upon her mind or body, before such an effect as this could have been produced. It is satisfactory in such cases to trace the accident to some known cause, if possible, if only to prevent the recurrence of anything so sad."

But Mr. William Treherne was quite unable to give Dr. Henderson any satisfactory reason for the destruction of the little life before them. Mrs. Treherne's feelings had not been sufficiently his care to enable him to say to what pitch they had been carried, or not. So the subject was waived.

"About breaking this news to Mrs. Treherne, Miss Salisbury? We wished to secure your assistance. Your sister might take it better from you than from another. Do you think it will be a great shock to her?"

Grace, remembering Elfrida's often expressed dislike to the idea of having a child to look after, and her often repeated wishes that it might never live, answered, as she believed, "No!"

"It will be a very good thing if it does not," was the doctor's reply, "as Mrs. Treherne is disposed to be feverish, and it is highly necessary that she should not be agitated. She is asleep now, and will probably sleep some time, as she has had an anodyne; but when she wakes, the sooner she knows it the better. It is no use dissembling on such subjects. With your permission, Mr. Treherne, my friend Dr. Hard wick will leave for the present, but I will stay here until Mrs. Treherne wakes, and I can judge of the progress she is making."

They were preparing to leave the room when Grace stopped them with a motion towards the infant.

"Oh! Dr. Henderson, can nothing be done? must it really die?"

He was beginning to answer her gently, when William interrupted him.

"Of course not, Grace. How can you ask such a question? As it is, I think it a very good thing that it must."

There was a look very much like disgust in the faces of both the doctors at his remark; but Dr. Henderson only answered Grace's question.

"Nothing, my dear Miss Salisbury. The injuries are internal as well as external. You must be satisfied that there is no suffering. A few hours at the most will end its life: we can do nothing but watch it."

"Poor little baby," said Grace, whilst her tears fell fast.

The doctor made no reply to her remark: he only bowed as he left the room with the other gentlemen. Then Grace was left alone with the nurse, and the two women bemoaned the little crippled frame—so crippled that it was impossible to dress it in frock or bedgown made for ordinary infants—and lifted the flannel every minute or so, to see if the quick, faint breathing was continued, whilst they talked in low whispers of the mysterious little life which had only been lighted up to flicker out again.

"Hush!" said Grace suddenly, when some time had elapsed, "hush, nurse! I heard something!" They listened with their breaths held, and a low call of "Grace," came from the next room, where Elfrida lay.

"I must go," said Grace; "oh, what shall I say if she asks me!" As she entered her sister's bedroom, and crept softly round the closed bed curtaius, till she came to the side where Elfrida lay, she could scarcely believe that the happy, peaceful face she saw before her was the same she had left with knitted brows, and clenched hands pressed against her mouth to stifle her own cries. Elfrida was awake—languid and pale, but awake, and looking very happy and contented.

"Oh, Grace dear," she said, " I want to see you so much. I want to tell you how wicked I have been and how happy I am. I have got a darling baby; I know I have, because I heard it cry as they took it out of the room. Oh, Grace, how good of God to send me a live baby, when I have so often been so wicked and said I hoped it would never be born! How little I deserve His goodness! Dr. Henderson thought 1 was asleep; but I have been lying here thinking of my happiness and of God's mercy in bringing me safely through that horrible pain, and giving me a live baby. Oh, Grace, I want to see it; I want to kiss my baby, and tell it, when I said I didn't want to have a child, I didn't know how dear it would seem to me directly I heard it cry. My dear little baby: how I shall love it! Is it a boy, Grace, or a girl?"

"A boy, dearest Frida," said Grace, sadly.

"Is it pretty, Grace? Oh! I want to see it. It seems so strange that I should have a child of my own and not have seen it yet. Why did nurse take it into the next room? Tell her to bring it here. A little boy! a little son! Oh! I am so thankful."

Her cheeks were flushed, her eyes were wet with tears, as she raised them gratefully towards Heaven. Grace was appalled at her words and her anxiety.

"Not yet, dear Frida; you had better not see it yet. You are still too weak and ill."

"Oh! no; not too weak to see my own baby. Tell them to bring it and put it in my arms, and I will go to sleep directly, I promise, Grace."

"Wait till I ask Dr. Henderson, Frida," said Grace, anxious to gain a respite, and for that purpose her sister let her leave her. Then she flew down stairs breathless, and bursting into the dining-room, where Dr. Henderson sat, told him of her sister's eager request.

"Oh, Dr. Henderson, what is to be done? Must I tell her?"

"I am afraid so, Miss Salisbury, unless Mr. Treherne could do it better."

But Mr. Treherne declined to have anything to do with so unpleasant a task.

"The sooner it is done the better, Miss Salisbury; certainly before she sees the infant; and then, if she is very agitated, I will administer another sedative to her afterwards."

So poor Grace retraced her steps sadly to Elfrida's side, wishing she could save herself from the task before her— by the severance of a hand or a foot.

"May I have it?" asked Frida, eagerly, as she re-entered the room. "Does the doctor say I may?"

"Presently, dearest Frida, if you will be quite quiet and good; but promise me not to agitate yourself. Would you be very sorry, darling," said Grace, coming close to her sister's side, and laying her head on the pillow beside her, "very sorry, if you had no little baby?"

"Oh, Grace—of course I should. I dare say you hardly believe me, because I was sinful enough before to say I should be glad to have none—but I did not know then, I did not know," she added, placing her hand upon her bosom, "that I should *feel* so when it was really born. Oh, Grace, tell the nurse to bring it quickly!"

"Frida, dear, we are all disappointed sometimes; God sends us disappointments for our good, doesn't He?"

The young mother's fears were roused now, and she said, "There is something the matter, Grace; my baby is dead, and they have not told me." And then Grace, with her arms about her sister, told her, as gently as she could, that the baby was not dead, but that God had seen fit to afflict it, so that it could not live for many hours. The crimson flush on Elfrida's face faded through all the stages of pink and ashen grey to a dull white as she listened.

Then she said, wearily, as her sister concluded, "Only a few hours?—Grace, tell the nurse to bring him here at once. Why did she keep him from me a minute?" And when Mrs. Meade, summoned, brought the roll of flannel into the mother's bedroom, and laid it by her side in the bed—as she expressed herself afterwards—"The sight was enough to draw tears from a stone." As Elfrida was about to uncover the little baby's body, Grace said, nervously—

"Don't look at it, dearest Frida, only look at its fece; you will distress yourself." But Frida said, "I wish to see it," and persevered in her intention. When she had uncovered it, she looked in silence, long and deep silence, at every part of the little crippled frame. Then she bent over and kissed, with a reverent tenderness, the tiny deformed limbs, kissed them softly, and yet with a passion, apparent in her eyes; and then folded the wrappers about it again, leav-

ing only the quiet baby face visible, and laid it close against her bosom, encircled by her arm. When she spoke, it was very quietly, and without tears.

"Grace, how did this happen?"

"What, dear T

"What has killed my baby?"

Her sister almost feared to answer her, but she repeated her question, and almost imperatively.

"You must know. What did the doctors say?"

"They think it must have been some shock, dear sister, to your mind or body—some mental strain. Perhaps it was poor dear mamma's death, Frida, or your own health. It is God's will, my darling. Be my own dear Frida, and try to submit to it quietly."

"I am going to," she answered. "Some great shock was it—some mental strain? Grace, tell the nurse to go away, and you stay with me alone."

And so Mrs. Meade, although she strongly objected to leaving the room without the baby, was obliged to submit and to retire.

"Don't talk to me, Grace," was Frida's request as soon as they were left alone. "Sit by my side, with your hand in mine, and let me look at my poor baby and think."

So she lay for some time gazing and thinking. But when it was apparent that her infant's hours were closing, and Grace called the nurse and doctor, and it was thought right to take the child from her, Frida's unnatural calmness gave way. "Grace," she almost screamed, " don't let them take it away! my murdered baby! Oh, Grace, I have killed my baby— it is all my fault! How could I tell I should love it, and it would die? Oh, doctor, give me back my baby. It is I who have killed it—I, its own mother, killed it! Oh, my little baby, my little boy, I should have loved you so!" Then her agitation, which Dr. Henderson's sedatives were unable to quiet, brought on the fever which they had dreaded for her, and nine or ten anxious days on the part of those who loved her followed; and in the meanwhile the poor little baby passed away and was buried and forgotten, in the more important work of watching over the mother's life. But at the close of that time, Elfrida was pronounced out of danger, and her recovery thenceforward was steady, though slow. She never mentioned her baby again, even to Grace, but she would sit for so long a time silent and absorbed, during those hours of convalescence, in the quiet darkened dressing-room, that Grace was only too glad of any piece of intelligence to tell her that might rouse her from her dreams. And, in consequence, it was with greater cheerfulness than she would have used on the subject, some time back, that she told her sister one day that she had just seen Captain Treherne.

"He has inquired for you, dear, almost every day, and has seemed very anxious to see'you. He asked to-day how soon you would be able to receive visitors, and I told him I would ask you. I think it would do you good to see your friends sometimes now if we could get you down into the drawing-room. Will you try to-morrow, dear Frida?"

Frida's eyes, looking so large from the alteration of her face, had been turned with a wistful anxiety upon Grace as she first mentioned George Treherne's name; and at the close of her words, instead of objecting vehemently to seeing any one as she had been accustomed to do of late, nor yet with any visible agitation of manner, she said with a quiet resolution, as if it was a duty that she must submit to—

"Yes, Grace, I will go into the drawing-room tomorrow and see Captain Treherne. I want to speak to him alone for a few minutes." And then without further allusion to her reasons for so wishing, she turned the subject, and did not mention it again. But she did not forget it, for the first thing she reminded Grace of the next morning was, that this was the day that she was to try and get down to the drawing-room floor. When her removal was accomplished, and she was laid upon the sofa, looking so white and thin and weak, Grace was afraid the exertion had been almost too much for her, and urged her making no further one for that day.

"Don't see Captain Treherne to-day, dear Frida. Leave him till to-morrow; the interview will be too much for you."

But her only answer was, "No, thank you, Grace; I would rather see him to-day. I have something to say to him."

When he called at his usual time, and was shown by Mrs. Treherne's order into the drawing-room, Grace was sitting with her sister. George Treherne's entrance was hurried and his action nervous; he looked very pale; but when he found that Elfrida was not alone he sat silent, not knowing what to say, because his heart was so full. The alteration which the cruel wasting fever had made in her struck him to the quick, connecting, as he could not but connect the change, with the last interview they had had together in that very room. Elfrida appeared as if she scarcely dared raise her eyes to his, and the fingers with which she attempted to pursue some trifling work trembled visibly. Grace saw their mutual embarrassment; and feeling herself *de trop,* she presently rose under some trivial pretence, and left the room. Then George's yearning eyes, full of a renewed tenderness, sought Elfrida's, and looked for the response he had never yet missed from hers; but it was not there. Elfrida's eyes were still bent upon her work. Then he spoke out and passionately—

"Elfrida, it was not I who brought this upon you. Tell me, it was not I—I have suffered so dreadfully all through it. I would have laid down my life to save yours." VOL. III. c

His tones were so earnestly beseeching, that they almost brought the tears into her eyes; but she made a violent effort, and restrained them.

"It was not you, George," she said, gently. "It was God's will, and His chastisement to me for all I have done wrong; I am sure it, is, though I can hardly see my way clearly yet. But I have been thinking a great deal, George, whilst I have been lying ill—thinking of you."

"Dearest!" he said with emphasis, but a look of pain passed over her face at the words.

"And of our last conversation together," she went on to say. "George, it must not be—it must never be again!"

"What?" he asked, "what must never be again?"

"We have gone too far," she said, taking no notice of the question. "I have been to blame, I know, as well as you; but I was so happy in your love and sympathy, and so unhappy in my own life, that I forgot, I never dreamt what it might lead to. I thought we should go on being friends for ever, and nothing more."

"Oh, forgive me, Elfrida," he exclaimed. "Dearest, you are right; I was mad to speak to you as I did. We will be friends for ever, Frida—friends as we were before. I will never offend or vex you again as I did on that wretched day. Don't you believe me T "Yes, I believe you, George. I felt for you as much as for myself when I found I was so ill, because I was sure you would think it was partly your fault; but that is not what I want to make you understand. It is very hard to say," she added, whilst the tears, which would not be longer restrained, fell fast upon her lap, "but I must say it. George, we must not even be friends; at least, not as we have been—we must give up seeing one another altogether."

"Good God, Frida!" he exclaimed; "you don't know what you are saying—your illness has weakened you frightfully."

"I know it has," she returned; "but I am strong enough to go through with what I feel to be my duty. It is no light duty, George. I have permitted myself to care for you until, if God were not with me, I could not say what I have said and mean it. But I do mean it. I have allowed 'the interest I feel in you to turn my inclinations and my steps from all home duties. I lived as in a dream until you awakened me. How must I have lived to have made such an awakening necessary to open my eyes?"

"Frida, I have said it shall never be again."

'"There will be no opportunity," she answered. "The evil has not ended there, George—my child was crippled and killed by my own wicked indulgence of feelings I ought never to have had."

"Is it possible?" he asked, in a low voice. "You must be mistaken."

"Mistaken!" she said, her agitation rising with her subject. "Ask Dr. Henderson if I am mistaken. He said so—he said a mental shock or strain had been the cause, that I am now a mother without a child. George, when I saw its poor little crippled body, and knew it had been injured by the violence of my own feelings, I promised that if God raised me up from my sick bed again, I would break off with you once and for ever."

"Once and for ever," he repeated sarcastically; "that is easier said than done. Is your love such an easily-disposed of commodity that you can give that up, at the same time, once and for ever?"

"Oh, no!" she answered sadly, "I know I shall bear that as a heavy weight to my life's end. I cannot give that up, it is part of myself; but the other I must and will! George, help me to do right! *Tell* me to do right, and it will be easier. I have brought this burden upon myself by my own folly— but, having brought it, I must bear it. It may be harder and heavier than I expected; it is—but does that alter the fact? My duty is plain before me. I would persist in doing it, were it ten times harder than it is. I dare not live longer in the temptation of enjoying your friendship. I will not trust myself or you. I *could* have cared for you—George, you know I could have cared for you, as I could have cared for no one else—but it must not be. The temptation is too strong, or I am too weak. If we continue to be to each other what we have been, God knows where it might end."

"Oh! I wouldn't trouble myself about that," he answered; "you seem to have no difficulty in altering your feelings exactly to suit the circumstances surrounding you. I should think there was no fear for you!"

"Oh! George," she cried, "for God's sake, don't talk to me like that; you are stronger than I am. Don't make my task harder than it is."

Her voice was broken, though her feelings were too strong for tears. She was unable through weakness to rise from the recumbent position in which she had been placed; but as she lay there, fragile and pale as she was, she looked the better man of the two. There was a heroism sparkling in her eyes, the spirit of a martyr breathing from her lips, which should have touched a man's heart with admiration for the virtues which she emulated, if he could not sympathise with the necessity for their exhibition. But George Treherne, if he did admire, would not acknowledge that he did so. He was immoveable, and stood his ground.

"I do not ask you for more than friendship," he said; "you have allowed me to care for you for months, and professed to care for me in return. Now, because you happen to be weak and out of sorts, you want to cast me off like an easy glove, and forbid me even to have the privilege of seeing you as a friend, or speaking to you. I have suffered a great deal for you, Elfrida; I was prepared to suffer a great deal more; but I did not expect this at your hands."

"What shall I do? what shall I do *T* Her face was buried in her hands, her whole frame shook with her emotion.

"Do you love me, Elfrida?"

The question had been asked hundreds of times before; but when are lovers tired of asking it? But now it seemed to rouse all Elfrida's indignation.

"Are you a man," she exclaimed vehemently, "to sit there and torture me with such a question? You know the answer well enough; but T will not give it you! I have made a promise to God, and I will keep it. It is the only reason for which I asked to see you here to-day. From this hour our intimacy is over. We may meet occasionally, but never in private—never as we have met before."

"If it is to be never as it has been before, it shall be never at all," he answered, angrily. "Your friendship, affection, whatever you may choose to call it, might have made a better man of me in time. Now, whatever happens to me, you may lay it at your own door. Don't be surprised if you hear I drink, gamble, do anything, or everything. I have no principle. You were my God and my religion, Elfrida: you cast me off and I have none. I did think you were beginning to teach me to respect better things, if I did not love them; but you have undone your work, if you ever did; you will send me from you desperate. If I go straight downwards, remember, it is your fault!"

"Oh! no, George—not that! for God's sake, don't say that—I, who am tearing my own heart this day to save you from wrong. Oh! go on thinking of better things until we meet again in heaven. George! this life is not for ever; we shall meet again, when the misery of this world is over."

"Not if we part now," he answered, sternly. "Elfrida, if you have one desire, however feeble, to see me again after this life, keep me by you now."

"I cannot; I dare not," she answered.

"This is your final determination?" he asked, rising.

"Yes," she said, resolutely, though her voice trembled, "it is my final determination. If I was told this moment that I should never see you again, I could but say the same. As intimate friends, as lovers, we must part to-day, and for ever."

"Then good-bye," he said, moving towards the door. "I go, but you send me away with the devil in my heart. God only knows how or when we may meet next."

She felt as if her powers of utterance were gone, she could only watch him as he went. When he reached the door, he turned his head once more and said—

"Is it really your final answer? Elfrida, consider, in another moment I shall be gone."

"Really and truly," she answered (but her eyes looked through him as she spoke, as if she wished in that moment to take in an impress of his figure which should last her for a lifetime). "What could I say otherwise? what could I do? Between you and I there falls the shadow of God." Then the door slammed and he was gone.

"God bless him," she moaned in the agony of separation. "God bless him and keep him from evil! I would have loved him. I would have died for him, if I might; but I have only done my duty. Heaven help us both! he to bear it bravely, and I, to live."

"Grace," she said to her sister when she returned to her side a short time afterwards, "put me to bed again, I cannot sit up any longer." And then when she was undressed and on her bed, she threw her arms about her neck, before she left her to repose herself, and whispered in her ear with a tightened grasp of her hand—

"Grace, darling, my life seems over; everything that was worth living for, to me, is past and gone— past and gone for ever. Oh, sister, I wish I was with mamma and baby in heaven!" CHAPTER II. MR. TREHERNE GETS HIS OWN WAY.

Helene Du Broissart had not felt very comfortable after her interview with John Eead. It had had no power to affect her; but it had had the power to alarm her. She felt no pity for the wounded and deceived heart of the man she had professed to care for; no renewal of tenderness had stirred in her breast as he reminded her of the days at Chelton-Marsh, when they had been all in all to one another. But his words and his threats had frightened her, because she saw that he was in earnest, and she felt that what he said he meant. But her alarm only lasted for a short time. When she came to remember his station in life and his appearance, and to contrast it with the wealth and power which surrounded her at Ariscedwyn, she was inclined to laugh at her own fears that he could possibly hint her or hers, even if he wished it. So the feeling gradually died away, and Helene put away the recollection of John Eead from her as an unpleasant one; or if she did think of him and his recent visit,,it was rather to wonder at his presumption and effrontery than at her own coldness of heart and shortness of memory. He, a labouring man, dressed in common fustian clothes, a fisherman, or whatever he might be now, to suppose it likely Mademoiselle du Broissart would leave all her newly-found relations to go back to CheltonMarsh with him, and to live in a hut on the beach! It was an absurd notion, as the world goes; but John Eead

had seen very little of the world, and he had seen a great deal of Helene's heart, or what she swore was such. But she never had a heart, and all the feeling, his deep feeling excited in her, was fear for her own annoyance, and dread of discovery. If she could have heard the next day that the body of John Bead had been found drowned in the canal, she would have only felt very thankful to think he was out of the way, and would trouble her no more. She hated the remembrance of the love-passages which had passed between them, and no one feeling of compassion animated her bosom for his constancy or his distress. She only wished never to see him again. She compared his appearance with that of her cousin, Captain Treherne; and since she did not love him, he naturally lost by the comparison. She was a little shy at first of renewing her usual afternoon rides, and her horse was permitted to stand idle in his stable for some time after her interview with him; but gradually, as the thought of his threats died out of her mind, she resumed her accustomed exercise. She need not have feared meeting him again; John Read had another purpose in his breast now, and his footsteps had been turned far away from Blackheath. As the Christmas holidays approached, Miss Plimpton had to find fault several times with Mademoiselle du Broissart for undue levity, boisterousness of manner and behaviour, and inattention to study, all of which reprimands were brought down upon her in consequence of a letter received from her grandfather, in which he told her that her cousin, Captain Treherne, had promised to spend his Christmas with them at Ariscedwyn; and Helene, quick to interpret any advances on his part as marks of special favour to herself, immediately ascribed his acquiescence in the proposed visit to a desire on his part to see more of her than he had done. The young ladies of the College returned to their respective homes about the middle of December, and Helene du Broissart had been some days at Ariscedwyn when George had the interview with Elfrida which I have described in my last chapter. When he had

left her presence, with oaths upon his tongue, and, as he said himself, the devil in his heart, he caused his necessary articles of clothing to be packed, and threw himself without further thought into a train for London—left Milborough without a farewell to either sister or mother, with no hint of his intention to Captain Digby, or any other friend, and cast himself without one safeguard, with no other guide but the devil in his heart, into the very midst of the temptations of the town. There he passed a week, which I must not describe to you—a week during which he disgraced his manhood by excess of every kind— in which he strove hard to efface the impress of God's image stamped upon him, in which he tried to drown care by brutality, and deaden conscience by the lowest and most sensual pleasures— a week to which he looked back afterwards with sorrow and shame, in which he was mad, debased, not human, anything rather than himself. Then when it was over, when his cup of dissipation was drained, he crept onwards to Ariscedwyn; not flushed, excited, and desperate as when he left Milborough, resolved to kill himself with vice if he could, or so deface himself that *she* should not know him again, but low in spirits, feeling degraded, unfit to hold up his head amongst his fellow-men; and yet still hardened, and with a dogged sullenness in his purpose, which I doubt was ever seen before on the face of George Treherne. He had given his uncle no notice of his coming, but he was expected about that time, and therefore his arrival was the occasion of no surprise. He walked in at the time that every one reached Ariscedwyn, about five or six o'clock, and was just in time to join his uncle and cousin Helene at the dinner-table. His appearance seemed to afford them mutual satisfaction, but his own manner was grave, downcast and subdued; so unusual a mood in him lately, that Mr. Treherne, through all his pleasure at meeting his nephew again, could not but notice it. Nothing was said upon the subject, however, during the evening. Inquiries were made and freely answered respecting the various families at Sorel Cottage, the Lawn, and Crossley; the face of the country, and the appearance of crops was discussed, the latest news of the day retailed, but no allusion was made to a subject of so private a nature as the visitor's state of mind or spirits. Helene was bois terously pleased to see her cousin, and assailed him so continuously during the evening with fulsome attention or flattery, and when she found that failed, with such open though silent expression of her feelings towards him, that it was no wonder he looked thoroughly wearied by the time that young lady thought fit to leave him in peace and take herself off to bed. Then as he sat alone with his uncle, over, their parting glass, a thin curl of smoke from George's cigar alone intercepting their faces, as they sat opposite to one another, he unburdened his mind of its load and spoke. Mr. Treherne gave him an opening, by saying,

"I am glad you came down so soon, George; I scarcely hoped for you before Christmas eve."

"Nor should I have come so soon, uncle," was the answer, "only I had something to say to you."

"I saw there was something wrong, my dear boy, when you entered," said Mr. Treherne, compassionately. "Tell me what worries you, George—is it money? You know you can always have as much as you wish from me. If it is"

"My dear uncle," said George, moved by the old man's evident affection, "I know you have always been the kindest of relations to me, almost like my own father; if I was in any scrape, I should never hesitate to apply to you for help; but it is nothing of the sort. I don't know why I should look hipped, or feel so, for the subject I came to speak to you on ought to be a happy one; I believe, at all events, it will please you, and that is all I care about. You remember, sir, speaking to me, now a year and a half ago, about a marriage between Mdlle. du Broissart and myself?"

"I do, George," returned the old man; "I have often been sorry since I was so hasty, I did harm instead of good. You must forget it, my dear boy, you must

forget all about it. I would not force your inclination now, if I could, nor hers either. It was a mistake of mine—a great mistake."

"Would you not wish such a marriage to take place now, then, sir ?

Mr. Treherne took off his spectacles nervously, then put them on again, and stared at his nephew.

"Wish it—of course I would—if it were possible; it has been the greatest wish of my heart; but I have given up all hopes of it, George."

"You should never despair, uncle," returned the younger man, with a reckless dash at gaiety, "for the reason which brings me down to Ariscedwyn tonight is to propose for the hand of Mdlle. Helene du Broissart. I have thought over your wish often, and I have come to the conclusion that it will be the best thing I can do to take your advice. If my cousin is willing to accept me as her husband, and you are willing to give her to me, I will marry her when you like, and the sooner the better." And George Treherne, having drained his glass of brandy-andwater, filled up another, stiffer than the first. Mr. Treherne was so taken by glad surprise that he could not at first answer his nephew, he thought he must be in a dream, to hear him really and truly accede to this long-cherished wish of his own. He was not a fond father, like Dr. Salisbury, anxious to ascertain first if the man who wished to marry his heiress possessed her heart. He had come to like Helene; but George and the estate were far dearer objects of interest to him, and in this sudden proposal he thought not that the two creatures nearest related to him were about to become husband and wife, but that his nephew, whom he loved as a son— and the estate, which he loved "as himself—were to be united, as he had always hoped they would be—for ever. He gazed at George Treherne for a few minutes in silence, and then getting up from his chair, and, Vol. in. D many women had sighed for him in vain? Helene thought of the husband she had just accepted and the acres of Ariscedwyn, and heaved a long deep sigh of gratified ambition and content.

seizing the young man's hand, he said, in a choking voice—

"My dear boy—my dear George! I am so happy —I am so very happy!" and then broke down altogether. George drank off his second glass of spirits, and then sat with his eyes fixed upon the ground, in moody abstraction. Presently his uncle said, in a voice of sudden excitement—

"When shall the marriage take place, George? Helene, of course, cannot return to Miss Plimpton. I shall write at once to that lady and tell her of the child's approaching marriage; but when shall it be?"

"Whenever you and the lady like, sir," answered his nephew, carelessly. "Next week, if it's convenient, it's all the same to me; but you calculate too much upon Mademoiselle du Broissart's consent, I am afraid. I have not been a very attentive wooer, as yet."

"I *think* I can guess what the answer will be, George; but you can speak to her the first thing to-morrow morning, and make sure for yourself. Only, I think I may tell you a little secret now which I guessed long ago—that she has cared for you some time. I am an old man, you know, and she tells me of her little fancies; and I think—I think I can guess what *her* answer will be, George. "

George thought he could guess also, and shuddered at the thought; yet he remained unshaken in his determined purpose.

"At all events," he said to himself, as he prepared to undress for the night," I shall have Ariscedwyn to console me, and *she*"— but here his teeth clenched, and an ominous stamp upon his bedroom floor resounded through the silent house—" *she* shall repent her cursed prudery, which withdraws even friendship from me as too much."

The interview with Helene in the morning was not long. She had been prepared for it previously by her grandfather, and was awaiting George in the diningroom when he descended to breakfast, all blushes and broad smiles and awkward confusion. But his manner was so very collected and business-like that it would have chilled the warmth of any heart more susceptible of manner than Mdlle. du Broissart. He advanced towards her, without any pretence or show of love-making, and shook her hand. Then he said—

"Helene, I suppose my uncle has told you (as he said he would) the substance of my conversation with him, last night. I have come down here earlier than I intended, for the express purpose of asking you to be my wife. Do you say yes, or no?"

"Now don't, George," she said, in a giggling school-girl manner, especially abhorrent to him. "I've never thought of such a thing, I'm sure."

"You can think of it now," he answered, gravely. "You must know your own wishes on the subject, and you must be led by them. Do you wish it *I 'Do you?"* she asked in answer.

"Yes, or I should scarcely be here. Helene, say one thing or another. Don't keep me waiting."

Then she said yes, and tried to look very modest over it, and drew herself closer towards him, as if she expected a renewal of the tender embraces she had been used to receive from her first lover. But nothing of the sort came. George Treherne took her hand, and said simply—

"Thank you, Helene. I am afraid my courtship has not been conducted in a sufficiently orthodox style for my offer to deserve so ready an acceptance at your hands; but I must try to make up for it now. I think my uncle must be waiting to come to breakfast until he hears that I have spoken to you. I will go and tell him that our interview is over."

And then he quietly kissed *her* forehead and left the room.

She stood, when he had left her, all in a glow of delight at the good fortune which had befallen her. Her thoughts did not rest tenderly on the idea that she was to be all in all to the man she loved—his wife and his life companion. Helene du Broissart's love was of the head, not the heart; she had no heart—no more for this elegant and accomplished Captain Treherne than she had had, for rough, but joving, John Eead,

in the days of old. She was delighted at the prospect of marrying this one, for the same reason that she had once been delighted at the prospect of marrying the other, because she loved—not them, but power and admiration, and a certain place in the world. Once she revelled in the idea of enchaining the handsomest fisher-boy on the coast; now she revelled in the idea of becoming the wife of the admired and sought-after Captain Treherne; and the thought that Elfrida, the mad girl of the College, whom she fancied laughed at her—the beautiful bride, who usurped all her cousin's attention, and outshone herself in the domestic circle, and who had since almost monopolised the friendship of George Treherne—would be vexed and perhaps made jealous by his union with herself, tended greatly to enhance the pleasurable feelings she was indulging in. How

When her grandfather and cousin reentered the room, the former was full of bustling importance and pride. His talk through the whole of breakfast was all about the farm and pasturage land of the estate, to which his nephew listened with an uninterested, not to say weary look upon his face. Mr. Treherne seemed to have forgotten altogether that his granddaughter was still his heiress. With the knowledge of the approaching marriage, all the estate seemed in his eyes to have reverted to George, and George only, until at last even George, careless as he was of anything that concerned Helene, thought the constant allusion to himself as sole proprietor of the whole place rather premature, and sounding very much as if the marriage had been arranged solely for mercenary motives; which thought made him rise sooner from the breakfast-table than he would otherwise have done; but even then his uncle followed him.

"You'll go round the place with me, George, won't you? I shall be so glad to have you again, my dear boy, to consult. Young heads, they say, are better than old. I wanted to ask you what you thought about draining the lower meadows; the three home fields would make a noble piece of pasturage for the young stocK, if we could; and the covers want

sadly looking to. I am getting too old to look after them as I should. Those keepers want a younger hand and eye over them than mine. We were obliged to dismiss two of the under-keepers last month for poaching, and only one of their places filled yet. Barnes is getting careless too. I was obliged to threaten him with dismissal; but I believe he would do his work well under a more active master. Shall we look round the farm first, George?"

"My dear uncle, I am no farmer; I scarcely know turnips from potatoes."

"Ah! but you will now, George, you will now; you will sell out of the army at once, of course, and live at Ariscedwyn on your own. Almost your own, George—as good as your own. It won't be long first."

"I hope it will be very long first," rejoined the younger man, with a sincere earnestness; "but I knew you would wish us to live at Ariscedwyn."

"Did you settle the time with Helene, George?"

"What time—of the marriage?"

"Yes."

"No, I did not mention it; but any time will do for me."

"Shall we say next month, then; the middle of next month, if practicable?"

"Yes, uncle, I'm ready; my trousseau will not take long preparing."

"Do you think your mother would take the trouble of procuring Helene's? The poor child having no mother," and then Mr. Treherne stopped, struck with a bitter memory. There was something, too, which rose in the younger man's heart, and threatened to choke him, but he stifled the feeling and replied—

"Oh! certainly; women always delight in shopping. I am sure you may make use of her in any way you like." "Would you prefer the wedding to take place at Milborough, George?"

George Treherne's foot came down with a heavy stamp—

"By heavens, no!" he exclaimed, and then recollecting himself, "I mean, of course, Mademoiselle du Broissart being your heiress, her marriage should take place from the estate."

"Oh yes, of course," said the old man;

"far better; I forgot that. Well, then, it is to be the middle of next month, George—that is a settled thing, eh?"

"Yes, the middle of next month."

George Treherne walked mechanically by his uncle's side that morning whilst he looked at farm operations, examined stock, admired the stables, and mentally weighed the pigs. His frame was carried along by the power of his will, but his heart was far away, spelling over a certain difficult lesson he had set himself to learn—" The middle of next month." It was not long, but it took him a long time to master it thoroughly.

Ariscedwyn, the loss of which he had so much lamented, was it possible it was to be his again, and that the knowledge could not interest him? He, who thought so much of luxury, and wealth, and this world's goods, was it possible that the anticipation of possessing all this fair estate, these noble acres and woods and covers, this thriving farm, that valuable house and its belongings, had no power to charm him, no power even to make him cheerful or feel content? No, the time had come when a smile, a look, a pressure from a woman's hand or eyes, had more charms for George Treherne than the wealth of the whole world. But no one guessed it but himself. From the bailiff, the coachman, and the gamekeepers, down to the grooms, the gardeners, and the farming-men, no one suspected but that the gay, careless-looking young gentleman, who sauntered about so easily and answered so lightly when addressed, was as happy a man as the earth possessed. And when they came to know that he was to be the possessor of the heiress and estate, they said amongst themselves that they did not wonder at his look of ease. They judged from his outward appearance only. You and I alone of them all can judge him by his heart. God save us from such ease!

CHAPTER III.

A NEW SERVANT AT ARISCEDWYN.

A Dull, murky afternoon in the middle of January; in the sky, leaden-coloured clouds, and a searching northeast wind, and at the door of the cottage of the principal gamekeeper of Ariscedwyn, the principal gamekeeper's fresh-looking daughter Bessie, looking fresher than ever as she shielded her face from the cutting wind with her apron, and looked from north to south, and from east to west, in the vain hope of catching a glimpse of her father's figure on his way home.

"There ain't no signs of him, mother," she said presently to some one inside the little room. "What can keep him out so late this bitter afternoon, and he without the muffatees I worked for him? Why, his fingers will be well-nigh nipped off with the cold."

"Father's got some extra work to detain him, Bessie, or he'd have been back to his fire-side before now. Why, it's nearly five o'clock. You come in from the door, my lass, or you'll get your death of cold."

But the girl did not heed her mother's warning.

"Five o'clock," she said, "aye; and it must be quite that, mother, for the workmen are beginning to put out their lights up at the Hall yonder. There must be plenty of work for them to do that they keep them at it byj their lanterns this kind of weather." And Bessie shuddered as she spoke.

"Well, there is enough of it, surely," answered the mother's voice; "what with papering and painting—inside and out—and the wedding day, not a fortnight off—it's as much as they'll do now to be ready in time"

"Only a fortnight!" said the girl, who had reentered the cottage again, and settled herself close by the fire; "I wonder how it feels, mother, to be going to be married in only a fortnight? I think the young lady up there cares more about it than the Captain does, any way, to judge by his looks."

"What makes you say that, Bessie? What have the likes of you to do with a gentleman's looks?"

"Can't I see?" laughed the girl. "Why, mother, they came along here together the day before yesterday, and Miss Brossart she was looking in the Captain's face—*under* his face, I call it, with them big eyes of hers, and he walked along the pathway as gloomy as you please; and when he answered her questions, he was quite short like, as if he was thinking of-something else."

"And perhaps he was, Bessie," was Mrs. Wyatt's reply, as she commenced laying her tea-table. "Gentlefolks have plenty to think of at times, and it's a serious thing, it is, to be about to take marriage on oneself."

"Ah, well," said the girl, saucily, *"if I was going to take marriage on myself, I shouldn't like my man to be thinking of anything but me, particularly when I was by him—and I wouldn't let him, that's more."*

"Well, well, Bessie," said the mother, laughing in her turn, "time enough for a little lass like you to settle such matters. You get the fork like a good girl, and make some hot toast against father's coming home."

But Bessie, making her pretty face crimson as she bent over the fire toasting round after round of toast for the better providing of the family tea-table, could not help pondering in her own mind why the young Captain, who seemed to have so much to make him happy in the prosperous future, should ever look downcast or gloomy or distracted. For George Treherne could not always keep up the gay, insouciante manner which he generally assumed in the presence of his uncle or his intended bride. He was generally in extremes, either recklessly gay or unusually silent and absorbed. These latter moods he reserved for his solitude, and under these circumstances his dependents had more than once observed and commented upon them. In the extensive alterations and improvements going on at the Hall he took no interest whatever. It was nothing to him if a bow-window was to be thrown out for the future Mrs. Treherne's dressing-room, or the wall knocked down between the library and study, or the roof of the house raised by two feet to heighten the upper ceilings. All the alterations were suggested by Mr. Treherne's agent, and carried into execution by Mr. Treherne's orders. No shadow of a wish or an idea came from the heir-expectant to all these honours. His uncle attributed his backwardness, in all but approval as the various works were completed, to his natural modesty and reluctance to appear to wish to further improvements of which he should reap the benefit; but he mistook the real reason. Bessie Wyatt was far truer in her judgment when she thought the Captain "didn't look somehow as he ought to look," and quite right when she hoped if ever she got a young man he might be less absorbed in his own thoughts and more in her as the marriage day approached. Heaven help the bright roses in Bessie's cheeks, if she lights upon a young man as little absorbed in his future wife as George Treherne was! As the girl pondered and toasted, and toasted and pondered, and the pile of toast grew alarmingly high upon the wooden platter on the table beside her, the January twilight, always so short, was suddenly lost in darkness, and the light of the fire was the only light in the room. "Here, Bessie," said her mother, suddenly re-entering the room, which she had quitted after her short conversation with her daughter, "look alive, girl. Here's father; it must be freezing again to-night, for I heard his voice ever so far off, and he's got some one with him—likely Drayton or Stokes. Set the door open, Bessie. Father never likes waiting for his welcome." And the good woman brightened up at the sound of her husband's approach till her face was a welcome in itself. Bessie started up from her reverie and he occupation at the same time, and throwing the last piece of toast on the top of her pile, set the cottage door wide open just as James Wyatt, the head gamekeeper of Arisccdwyn, and her father, was ready to step across it.

"Why, lass," he exclaimed, as Bessie's bright face beamed forth at him, "it's worth being out in the cold to come back to a home like this. Mother, have you a cup of tea for a stranger? it will be the first time in your life if you haven't." And so saying, James Wyatt stepped into his home circle, and showed the women that he had, as his wife had prophesied, another person with him. Not Drayton, though, or Stokes, but a perfect stranger; no one

they had ever seen before or heard of. But if Mrs. Wyatt's hospitality required any stimulus to excite it to action, this was just the thing to do it. A stranger, probably without friends, and on such a night.

"Of course, Wyatt," was her ready answer; "I shall always have a sup for a stranger, man, as long as you pays for it. Come in, my friend, and welcome," she added to the man himself, with a readiness which, if it was not graceful, was full of the milk of human kindness. "There's lots of toast Bessie's made for you, father, and I dare say our friend there won't mind a rasher after a day's work, and I'll get it ready in a twinkling."

The stranger she addressed did not make any reply, beyond a "Thank you kindly," but stood sheepishly behind James Wyatt, and as if he was rendered still more shy from the heartiness with which he had been received. He had removed his cap on entering the gamekeeper's lodge, and had disclosed a set of handsome, though sunburnt features. Now he made no movement forward, although kindly invited to do so by Mrs. Wyatt.

"Do sit down, now, by the fire," she said, cheerily; "it's a bitter night, and you must be well-nigh frozen. Sit you down, and have a good warm, while I cut you a rasher from our own bacon."

He accepted the offer by taking possession of a chair, but he made no further use of his tongue. As Mrs. Wyatt went into the back kitchen, intent upon cutting her rashers, her husband followed her there.

"Queer kind of customer, mother, ain't he? But he's new to the place as yet; and young."

"Who is he, father?"

"Well, he's applied for one of the under-keepers'

Vol. in. E places; he's not used to the work, being a labouring man, as he tells me, but anxious to better himself. I shouldn't have looked at him a few months ago, but Wilson's place has been vacant so long now, and Drayton complains of the night-work being too much for him, and master said to me,

'Get any one you can, Wyatt, for a temporary, and we can but change them if they don't suit.' But I fancy this chap will suit," added the gamekeeper, thoughtfully; "he's well made and strong, and has an honest look, through all his shyness. I brought him along with me, wife, because he came from the furthest town, and it's late to look for lodgings now in the village, and the ale-house ain't a safe rest for a young fellow like that. Could you manage a shake-down for him to-night out here, do you think?"

"I'll try," said Mrs. Wyatt, but with a certain degree of reticence, as she calculated in her matronly mind the possibilities of her doing so.

"I don't see how we can turn him out again," rejoined her husband, guessing her thoughts, "even if the Captain don't approve of Ins looks."

"Will the Captain be along here tonight, then?" demanded the woman.

"Sure to," was the answer. "He's out with Drayton, and one of the grooms, and he always goes home by the lodge, to leave the dogs. I'll catch Mm this, evening, and ask him to take a look at this chap."

"Ah, well! the Captain's sure to leave it to you, Wyatt. Ill get your friend a shake-down for tonight, any way; and you must help him to a lodging to-morrow."

As the husband and wife were discussing the newcomer's appearance, and taking an unnecessarily long time to cut the rashers of bacon, their pretty daughter was trying to make herself agreeable to him in their absence. So, after clearing her throat once or twice, and changing her position as often, she ventured to address him as follows:—

"You're new to these parts, ain't you?"

"Yes, I am," was the curt answer.

But Bessy was noways daunted.

"Are you likely to stop here long?"

"I can't say," the man replied; "it depends upon whether I'm hired here or not. I've applied for the gamekeeper's place."

"Oh! gamekeeper's place, have you? That's poor Wilson's; he died of fever last autumn; he caught cold being out at night. You should get the young Captain to speak to you; he'd be sure to engage you. He's such a good young gentleman."

"What young Captain?" inquired the stranger, with a degree of interest.

"Our young Captain—Mr. George; such a handsome gentleman! he as is to marry our young lady in a fortnight from yesterday. You will have just come in time for the wedding if you stop."

The face of the man she addressed grew darker under the pressure of her words, but he never spoke a syllable in answer to them; and the girl, unheedful of the impression she made, and brimful of her news, rattled on.

"The wedding's only been settled a month ago, and they've had a hundred workmen and more, up at the Hall ever since, making ready for it. It will be a grand sight. They say ladies and gentlemen are coming from ever so far to be at the church; and the bride's dresses are beautiful."

And then Bessie lowered her voice to almost a confidential whisper, as she incredulously added—

"Mrs. White, the lady's-maid at the Hall, told me she believed Miss Brossart had fifty silk gowns or more. Do you believe it?"

But the person she addressed, did not seem as if he even attempted to weigh the probabilities of the truth of this overwhelming statement. He merely asked—

"Does Miss—the lady you spoke of, often come down this way ?"

"No, very seldom," was Bessie's answer. "She never did at all, till she was engaged to the Captain; but since then, she has been two or three times, just to see him off shooting, like. This ain't so near to the Hall as you'd think by the lights; it's only because the trees are bare that we can see it at all. In summer it's quite hid by the leaves."

Here their conversation was interrupted by the return of Wyatt and his wife, with the rashers ready for the fire, upon which they were soon hissing, almost preventing talking by their noise,

and filling the little room with an odour more savoury than delicate. The party was now increased by the entrance of Wyatt's two sons—fine-grown lads of ten and twelve years old, who, with Bessie, completed the gamekeeper's family. The cooking of the rashers completed, they all sat down to the teatable, when Bessie's pile of toast rapidly disappeared down the throats of the Wyatt tribe; but the stranger ate little, and talked less.

"You don't seem to relish your food, friend," said Mrs. Wyatt, presently; "are you well?"

"Quite well, thank you," said the man, hurriedly, and commencing an attack upon the contents of his plate; "but I've, walked far to-day, and may be I'm over-tired."

"Ah! a good night's rest will set you all right," said the good woman, compassionately. "I never thought to ask your name yet. How do ycu call yourself, now?"

"Thomas Coles," answered the man.

"You're no relation to John Coles of Little New Htreet, in South Hackney, are you?"

The stranger shook his head.

"Ah! well, we're Londoners ourselves, you see; and living down in these wilds, as you may say, it's quite a treat sometimes to fall across a friend of old friends. Have you been in London lately?"

"I don't know it," said the stranger, apparently disinclined, for conversation. "I'm not from near those parts at all."

Mrs. Wyatt had it on the tip of her tongue to ask from which "parts" he was, when the sound of approaching footsteps along the frosty path, and of voices in the frosty air, made the gamekeeper leap from his seat and make for the door.

"It's the Captain going home," he said, in explanation; "you wait here, Coles, and I'll bring him along to speak with you." And leaving his lodge, he encountered the gentleman he sought, who, accompanied by a couple of men laden with his guns, and day's spoil, and followed by half a dozen dogs, was

giving some directions about their treatment, to the man who had appeared from the kennel, to receive them from him.

"Ah, Wyatt," he said, carelessly, as the gamekeeper appeared, "I was just telling Jim to tie up that bitch, and poultice her leg—she's hurt it in the brushwood; and don't let the pup come out with me again, he's very unsteady, and unsettles the others. James, you can go on to the hall."

"If you please, sir, might I speak with you a minute?" said Wyatt; and then proceeded to lay the case of Coles before the young Captain, and entreat him just "to look at the man," and give him his opinion.

"What good can I do by looking?" said George Treherne, wearily. "I know nothing about the fellows, Wyatt. You must find out if he's honest and does his work welL"

"Oh, I'll look after all that, sir, never you fear," was the gamekeeper's reply. "Only I should feel more easy, sir, if you'd just kindly see the man and speak to him; it would take some of the responsibility off my shoulders, sir; for the place is sadly in want of being filled, you see, sir, and the fellow seems likely. "

"All right," said George Treherne; "lead the way, Wyatt; I'll go in;" and following the gamekeeper into the sitting-room, found it deserted by all but the stranger Coles and Mrs. Wyatt, the young people having decamped at the instance of their mother to leave the coast clear.

"Good-evening, Mrs. Wyatt," said George Treherne, with his accustomed courtesy; "I suppose this is the man, Wyatt. Now, my good fellow, what's your name?"

They were a great contrast to one another; he, the bridegroom-expectant, the very ease of whose careless apparel bespoke him of the class who can afford to dress carelessly; his handsome face, paled by trouble and anxiety, looking more delicate and refined than usual, whilst he leant against the cottage wall with an air of fatigue that showed to advantage every proportion of his graceful figure—whilst before him stood the rustic clown, with a face and figure, perhaps, as fine by Nature, but spoilt from exposure and rough work, want of education and ill-fitting clothes. The stranger did not appear shy now, as he answered George Treherne's question, but rather sullen, which did not prepossess that gentleman, not gifted at any time with too much patience, in his favour.

"Speak up, man," he said quickly; "what did you say—Thomas Coles? Where do you come from?" "Hampshire."

"You don't talk like a Hampshire man; I am from there myself. What part of Hampshire did you live in?"

"Near Eomsey, sir."

"Well, that doesn't much signify. Who did you live with last?"

"With a farmer, sir, Farmer Crop; I worked on his farm."

"Ah, well," with a languid air, "you don't understand this sort of work, I suppose, but you must learn if you want to stay. You will be completely under Mr. Wyatt; he'll tell you all about wages and so on. Now, mind you're honest."

"I always am, sir," returned the man, hastily.

"Oh, very well, that's right! Wyatt, it's no use my talking to him any more, you can do the rest; good-evening, Mrs. Wyatt," and then, as the gamekeeper accompanied him to the door, he said, "He seems a sullen brute, Wyatt, but I should try him."

"I don't think he's naturally sullen, sir," returned the gamekeeper; "he's come off a long journey— and I think he's in distress, likely enough. The man seems more down, than sulky to me, sir, begging your pardon."

"Do you think so? poor devil," said George Treherne, pitifully, and then quickly re-entering the lodge, he said, as he put half-a-sovereign into Coles' hand, "You'll want something at first for a lodging, my man, but don't get drunk, we never allow that at Ariscedwyn." And then he took his way homewards, through the leafless park, with his eyes bent downwards, and his heart

still lower. When good Mrs. Wyatt had arranged the shake-down in the back kitchen, and the family had retired to rest, leaving the stranger to repose there as he might, he did not sleep well, though the bed was soft enough, the coverings amply warm, and he was very tired. He kept turning over and over from side to side, thinking of his interview with the young Captain.

"I told him I was honest," he thought to himself; "but it was a lie, when I had given him false answers all along. I wish he weren't so sad-looking, and so delicate, and I wish he had cut out my tongue before he had given me this money, and with them words, too. I wouldn't spend it on myself—no! not if I was starving of hunger or dying of thirst. I could have thrown it back in his face, only somehow lie don't look happy. Wait till I see them together, and then I expect I shall feel more towards him, as I ought to do." And the poor misguided creature, turning on his pillow, rapped out an oath against George Treherne, which he did not feel in his heart, even while it trembled on his tongue. But neither his oaths, nor his threats of vengeance, could stop the destiny which was coming upon the man he hated; and before the new under-keeper had fallen into the routine of his duties, the wedding bells had pealed for the marriage of Captain George Treherne with Mademoiselle Helene du Broissart. There had been a great concourse at the wedding and breakfast. Old Mr. Treherne, of course, in all his glory, as the giver-away of the bride, and Mrs. Henry Treherne, radiant with good-humour, as the mother of the happy bridegroom. Agnes acted the part of bridesmaid, in conjunction with Dora and Emma Treherne: the former young lady, who had given way to violent hysterics on the receipt of the news of her cousin George's engagement, having thought it just as well to have as much pleasure as she could out of the event, had consented to be bridesmaid, not without a latent hope that her loss even might be repaired, out of the number of eligible men she would meet there, from amongst the bridegroom's brother offi-

cers. Captain Digby, of course, was present; even Mrs. Henry Treherne's objections were overruled by George's steady determination that it should be so; and the Colonel, and several others—all right good fellows, and honourable gentlemen, who talked of the hospitalities of Ariscedwyn for many a day afterwards. Even William Treherne was present, with many a compliment for the bride, and apology for the absence of his wife, who was still unable to leave the house. The marriage went off splendidly; the ladies said that "dear Mademoiselle Broissart really looked 'very nice' under the white Brussels lace veil," and the gentlemen declared with one voice that "Treherne came to the scratch like a brick." If coming to the scratch like a brick, meant, going through the holy ceremony of marriage, without evincing the slightest feeling, perhaps the gentlemen were right; only Charles Digby ventured to whisper in Agnes' ear, when they had contrived to elude the vigilance of Mrs. Henry Treherne, and get a few minutes to themselves, after the married couple had taken their departure—

"Agnes, darling, I hope when you and I are married, that I shall look less grumpy than George did this morning. Does he profess to love that girl, or not
T

And Agnes had cried plentifully as she answered, clinging closely to her lover, "Oh, Charley dear, I hope he does; I do hope he does for his own sake; but I am afraid to think, or to say.
" CHAPTER IV.

THE LAST DROP IN THE CUP.

I Have not lingered long over the description of George Treherne's wedding, because in a former volume I have already given you the details of one as mournful, and you will begin to think I do not myself believe in happy marriages. But God forbid that I should say so. If my tale is so sad a one, that I am compelled in its course to tell you of foolish and rash acts, proceeding from the dictates of ignorant or undisciplined hearts, I tell them, because they were so, and I would be faithful, and not because I believe them to be the general course of action pursued by the world's inhabitants. To Elfrida, seated in her lonely house at Milborough, the sound of these mournful wedding bells could not reach. And yet she thought she heard them, throughout the whole of that winter's day. She was alone now, for her father had put his long-intended journey to

Scotland into execution as soon as she was convalescent, and Grace had gone with him. And so Elfrida was alone in reality to indulge her sick fancy as she chose. The news of George Treherne's intended marriage had come upon her as a second, and severer shock, than her voluntary renunciation of his love and friendship had proved. For throughout her resolutions, to break off her intimacy with her lover, she had carried, unknown to herself, a hope for the future. It had never entered her calculations that he would marry. She thought he would leave England, for years perhaps, and in her mind pictured herself and him, during that cruel time of separation, purifying themselves, and their affections, by regret for the past, until they should have schooled themselves to meet again, without so much as one throb that could denote the presence of a guilty passion, but ready to take up in its stead, a pure and lasting friendship for one another, which should endure to their lives' end. It had been a pleasant theme to dwell on, even in the midst of her first grief, which had even then the power of softening it, by the belief that the present trial might prove the salvation of her lover, as well as of herself. But when she heard of his engagement, all this airy comfort was dispelled. Here was a new view of the case. George Treherne married, and to a woman whom he could neither lore, nor she be friends with, was virtually separated from her for ever. He might as well—he might far better, have died at once, and faded from out the list of her living loves. Then he would have been still her own. Now, it seemed as if even the prospect of meeting him in heaven had lost its comfort. How did she know that, even in another world, Helene du Broissart would not still step between them, and

claim her own? Poor Elfrida! she had yet to learn, that they who hope to enjoy heaven, from the presence of any one but the King of Heaven himself, will find the entrance barred against them, and their vain desires. But as yet, her heaven lay in George Treherne's presence. She was shut out from it for a while, but the prospect of its future enjoyment was the only thing which kept her life within her. It had been better if her sister Grace had been with her on that wretched weddingday. To have been obliged to keep up some show of outward composure, would have been good for Elfrida, however painful. She could not, then, have shut herself up in her own room, torturing her heart by fancying, as each hour went by, what the wedding party were about. She would not have heard the false echo of wedding bells ringing out in the Milborough air, which were chiming no nearer than on the borders of Wales. She would not have had the leisure to imagine the triumph of the bride, the congratulations of friends, the ring upon the finger (at the thought of it, Elfrida drew off her own impatiently, and flung it on the ground), the name, passing from lip to lip, Mrs. George Treherne.

"Mrs. George Treherne!" was it possible that *he,* that George, had given any woman the right to bear that name, and be one with him? Poor heart! how it stood still, and shivered under the idea, too crushed even to cry out or to groan. If Grace had been there, Elfrida would have lain in her bed that night, whether she slept or not; and there would not have been, whilst George Treherne's blooming bride slept soundly by his side, a slight young figure, robed in its deep mourning, pacing restlessly up and down the bedroom floor, with a pale face, unwetted by tears, but with scared eyes peering into vacancy, and thin hands pressed against the throbbing brain, as if sense and life were passing away together. I wonder if any one else lay awake through the dark hours of that night! I wonder if any sympathetic heart guessed Vol. in. F too late the agony it had so suddenly inflicted, and had its rest broken by the thought!

I cannot tell, but I think it likely. When William Treherne returned to his home, a couple of days after the wedding, he found his wife in anything but the state he liked to see her. He was full of the scenes he had passed through; the descriptions of the various hospitalities and gaieties he had encountered, lost nothing at his hands, and Elfridamust listen and smile, and appear interested and pleased, or her husband lost his temper, and his patience with her.

"I declare, Elfrida," he observed the morning after his return, "you grow more seedy and lugubriouslooking every day. What on earth is the matter with you? I believe it's that horrid mourning that makes you look so pale. I always hated mourning, it's so unbecoming. You must leave it off. You've worn it six months, and I cannot endure it any longer. Pray come down in something more cheerful-looking to-morrow."

"Oh, William, let me wear it a little longer; not for poor mamma, I don't mean ihat, but for my poor little baby."

"For what?" exclaimed her husband, with genuine surprise.

"For little baby," said Elfrida, in a low, hesitating voice, for she knew the idea would be ridiculed by her husband. "I can't forget it, William, though it was only here so short a time. My black dress seems the only thing left, to remind us that we have had a child."

She had coupled their names together—she had spoken of " their" child, and the allusion would have had the effect of softening most men's hearts towards her; but the man she had to deal with was not like most men. William Treherne burst into a loud laugh as she timidly concluded her speech.

"You don't mean to say—" he chuckled, and then interrupted himself to laugh again, whilst the colour mounted painfully to his wife's pale cheek; "really, Elfrida, you must be taking leave of your seven senses—you don't mean to tell me, that you are dressing in black crape and bombazine, for the death of a child of a few hours' old—a child that couldn't have lived under any circumstances? By Jove, I couldn't have imagined you were such a fool. Incredible nonsense! But I believe it's only an excuse, because you know I hate the sight of black. Any way, you'll change it if you please."

"I'll change it at once," said Elfrida, haughtily for her pride was roused by her husband's ridicule, and, as she spoke, she rose to leave the room. "I see now, that I am foolish to regret the death of a son who might have followed in his father's footsteps." But before the words were out of her mouth, she was frightened at her own effrontery. The expression of William Treherne's face, changed from a sarcastic sneer, to a look of anger and almost dislike, as he sprang up from his seat and seized the trembling girl by the arm."

"You say that again, now!" he shouted in a coarse, brutal manner, as he grasped her arm so rudely that he hurt her; "just repeat those words, will you ?

"Oh! William—don't!" pleaded Elfrida, alarmed at his looks and action. "You said yourself there was nothing to regret."

"Trying to take refuge under a He, are you?" replied her husband, but without relaxing his hold. "This is what comes of your associating with your *dear* sister Grace. You are set against your husband's relations (you do not suppose your impertinent behaviour towards my mother and sisters has escaped my notice?), and taught to set up your will against his, and to look upon yourself as a most injured individual, and a wife to be pitied. I'll have no more of it. I'll let your canting old father, and that smooth hypocrite, Grace, know that they shall not come here conniving, and abetting your faults, for nothing—seconding you, in showing disrespect to my relations, and in opposing my wishes. Do you hear me, Elfrida ? and he shook the arm he held as he spoke.

"Yes, I hear you," she answered faintly; "but I deny the truth of what you say." Not the fear of his uplifted arm, deterred her from the acknowledgment, though it fell with no light weight upon her shrinking form.

"Go to your room," he said, pushing her out of the doorway; "if you behave like a child you shall be punished like one." But, as he re-entered the room, and heard the girl's footsteps slowly ascend the staircase, in obedience to his commands, and heard no word in return, no childish sob, to denote how much she felt his harshness, the man's triumph considerably faded; and, mean-spirited as he was, he felt himself to be what he was, a coward; and only hated her the more that she had betrayed him into showing himself one. He had acted upon an unfounded supposition, engendered by idle and illnatured repetitions; and, as he found himself alone, he felt that it was unfounded, and that he had acted foolishly. He felt in that moment, as the sound of his wife's footsteps fell fainter and fainter on his ear, that his hold upon her affections was dying away in like manner. He would have given much to have undone that hasty blow, and unspoken those hasty words; but he did not know the right way to go to work to remedy the evil. If he had had sufficient humility, at that moment, to have followed his wife, and made that one acknowledgment, "Elfrida, I was wrong, forgive me!" who knows, if that young bruised and bleeding heart might not, in its hour of loneliness and struggles after right, have poured its confidences out upon his bosom, and confessed the blight which had fallen upon their married life, and with the confession received strength to overcome it and to love again? Elfrida's heart was very sore, and in that hour, a few kind words from her husband might have cast her penitent at his feet, longing to cling to any love—even to his—to fill the void she felt within. But William Treherne was not gifted with humility. He saw his mistake, but he felt more disposed to resent it upon her, than upon himself. He cursed her in his heart, as he shut the diningroom door upon her retreating figure.

AndElfrida?

A second blow! She felt it keenly. The first had staggered her; but, after the first shock, she had come to persuade herself that it must have been a mistake—a passionate mistake, into

which he had been surprised, and that it could not happen again. But now it had happened again; and he had said she was a child, and should be treated as such. Was she to be beaten all her life, for everything she did wrong? Was she never to have a different opinion from her husband; never to be allowed to act for herself? Elfrida's thoughts for a moment flew to the idea George Treherne had presented to her, of what a life of love with him would be, and compared it to her stern reality; and, for a moment, she almost wished she had accepted his offer—only for a moment though—the next found her humbly on her knees, praying, "Oh! my God, forgive me for such a thought, and make me thankful that I am where I am!" But her prayer was almost mechanical, for even while she prayed, the uppermost feeling in her heart was hate against her husband. And whilst she felt as she did, and he continued to think, as we have last seen him, there was little chance of a reconciliation. William Treherne maintained an icy distance towards his wife, which each day seemed to increase instead of diminish, whilst Elfrida permitted herself to dream of her lost love, and compare its guilty pleasures, with the miseries of the lawful affection which was allowed her, till she persuaded herself, that it was no use attempting to live happily with her husband; and the only thing left for her to do, was to drag through life as best she might, and accept death when it came with gratitude. The marriage had taken place the latter end of January, and it was not until May, that the bride and bridegroom were announced to be on their way back from the Continent, and about to make a short stay at Sorel Cottage with Mrs. Henry Treherne, before they made a triumphal entry into Ariscedwyn. Three months had made a vast improvement in Elfrida's fragile appearance, although it had not seen much alteration in her spirits. The objectionable mourning had been laid aside, and with brighter colours, Elfrida looked brighter and less pale. But her look of youth was gone. Her twentieth birthday had not yet arrived, and yet no stranger would have thought of calling her a "girl." They might have said, and did, that "Mrs. William Treherne was a very sweet-looking young woman;" but they generally added, "only she looks very care-worn, or as if she had known a great deal of sickness." That was the general impression she made; but those who loved her, probably would have seen little difference in her, except that she looked delicate. A remembrance, a word, a look, that recalled the past, would flush her cheeks, light up her ardent eyes, call the caressing lines in play about her mouth, and she was "Elfrida" once more—the Elfrida of India—even of Blackheath. But such remembrances and moments were very rare. For a month before the George Trehernes reappeared in Milborough, little was heard amongst their relatives, but the account of the wonderful preparations that were being made in Sorel Cottage, for their reception. Agnes was constantly at the Lawn, with intelligence of the best bed-room having been fitted up with blue, for their accommodation, and herself turned out of her tiny bed-room to make it into a dressing-room for the bride.

"Mamma has never thought me worth a dressingroom since I was born," was her laughing assertion to Elfrida, as she narrated the history of her expulsion; "but nothing can be good enough for Mrs. George Treherne. That room looks so pretty, Frida, you really must come and see it, you wouldn't know it again. Mamma has had it repapered. She always meant to do it this year, and the dressingtable is a mass of white muslin and lace. I made such a lovely box-pin-cushion for her benefit also, with their crest in the centre. When will you come?"

"I am not very strong," faltered Elfrida. "I very seldom walk out; I will come if I can, dear Agnes; if not, you describe it so well that I can quite imagine how pretty it looks."

"It does indeed. I hope she will be pleased, because I don't think George cares much about such things. We expect them next week now, Elfrida. George wrote to-day. His letters are so

much more cheerful than they were. Oh, Elfrida! I was so afraid at first, that his heart was not in the marriage; but I really think I was mistaken. I think he is all right now, and I am so thankful!"

All right now! Yes; Elfrida tried to believe that it must be so. He had found it easier to forget than she had. Perhaps he had never even loved as she had. But she had prayed for this, and longed for it— that he might forget, and be happy. Then why should she regret if it was so? She did not regret it. She was thankful; she was happy. She said so to herself dozens of times, with the tears streaming down her face. All Milborough seemed anxious and interested in their return. Elfrida never met any of the officers of the 120th Lancers, but they stopped herself, or her pony phaeton, to inquire if any further news had been received, or if the day for the return was actually fixed, although their favourite Treherne no longer belonged to their corps. George had sold out of the army immediately after his marriage. It had been the express wish, and, indeed, stipulation, of his uncle, at the time of his proposals to Helene. At the moment he had acceded, indifferent to what he did; but when the time came for the actual resignation of a service in which he delighted, George had felt the fulfilment of his agreement with Mr. Treherne, to be a bitter aggravation of the lot he had taken upon himself. But it was the last drop in his cup of self-humiliation—the last price to be paid in exchange for the lands of Ariscedwyn. Everything had preceded it—so he told himself—love, honour, self-respect. The sacrifice of his profession was an atom in the scale. That resigned, he gave himself up solely, to be what he had vowed to be, the husband of Helene du Broissart, and the prospective owner of Ariscedwyn. How those weary months were dragged through upon the Continent he scarcely could tell for himself afterwards. They passed somehow, and he was thankful when they were gone, though England and France were alike indifferent to him. He did not even resent the notion of passing a week in Milborough on their way. Perhaps he thought it made

little difference, whether he saw Elfrida or did not see her. Perhaps he had a secret, gnawing, longing at his heart, only to see her once again, even if no words passed between them. Anyway, they came. William Treherne was very particular that his wife should not be backward in showing courtesy to the bride, and urged her making an immediate call. She did not resent his wish: she knew that she must see her, and endure her presence, sooner or later It was easier to do so during a formal morning visit, than in circumstances of greater intimacy. And yet it was an intense relief to her, as she waited tremblingly at the door of Sorel Cottage, for the answer to her knock, to hear the welcome words, as she asked for Mrs. George Treherne (how hard it seemed for her lips to form the words!), "Not at home, Ma'am; all gone out for the day." It seemed like a respite from-some fearful pain, which had seemed but the moment before, to be inevitable. Elfrida drew a long breath, almost a sob, as the green doors of Sorel Cottage closed again upon the servant, and she turned her pony's head in the direction of the country. A drive down the country lanes, redolent now of spring odours, and lined with hedges bursting into hawthorn blossoms, would soothe her, and do her good. But as she was proceeding quietly down one of her favourite haunts, a green shaded road, which had been a constant witness of her summer rambles, in company with one with whom she should never ramble more—(did the thought strike her, as she turned her pony's head that way?)—she saw a sight, which caused her to come to a sudden check, and then a quick retracing of her road, which quite upset the gravity of the spirited little animal she drove, and made the boy who sat behind her, with a vain assumption of the dignity of a full-grown groom, wonder " what on earth had come to Missus," and to express an opinion afterwards in the servants' hall that she was " mad as a 'atter." It was a little thing to alarm her, only the sight of a solitary figure, quietly walking many paces in advance of her carriage —

walking under the hedge, and smoking as he went. But her quick eyes had recognized him, even at that distance, and her quick heart pondered on the circumstance of his being there, and alone, and tried to get at the truth of it. The ladies were out for the day, and the bridegroom—the happy man—just returned from his wedding tour, was not with his bride, and mother, and sister, but wandering about, thoughtful and alone, in the solitary, unfrequented spot in which *they* had so often walked and talked together, in the days of the past! It was a dangerous subject for Elfrida on which to question her heart, and surmise—it was a subject, the reason for which, she could not analyse, without bringing a brighter glow to her cheek, and a softer light to her eyes, than had been there for many a day; and the blessing which she daily asked for him in her prayers, never seemed more sincere, or fervent, than it did that night, as the mention of it recalled that thoughtful figure alone in the solitary lane.

Elfrida had hoped, that, in the return call which she daily expected the bride to pay her, she might be equally fortunate" in missing her; and for that purpose ordered her carriage regularly after luncheon, and drove herself out, away from Milborough. But she was doomed to be caught. One afternoon, just as she had returned from her drive (for the evenings were still chilly, and she could not remain out late), and was about to take off her things in her own room, her maid brought the announcement that "Captain and Mrs. Treherne" were in the drawing-room. In a moment, Elfrida was white as death, and trembling all over; but there was no escape; she had not yet laid aside her hat and cloak, and she descended to the drawingroom as she was, trusting the former might aid in concealing the emotion she felt. As she entered the room, Helene sprang up, all bustle, pomp, and confusion, to receive her, with apologies for being so late, but they had such a number of visits to pay.

"George," she cried, in her loud, boisterous tones, to her husband, who was standing by the mantelpiece, his face rather turned away, "don't you see Mrs.

Treherne? Lor, my dear! I suppose I must call you Mrs. William, to make the difference, there's such a lot of Mrs. Trehernes now. We shan't know which is our own husbands if we don't take care." And she laughed aloud as she spoke.

He came forward and shook her hand, but Elfrida could not have told you afterwards, how he looked, or what he said. He said something though, about being glad to meet again, or some such commonplace, but the hands unclasped again without so much as a pressure, and the eyes never met. Elfrida was thankful for the fast-coming dusk, as she turned again to the bride— "I was sorry to miss you when I called." The conventional falsehood came from trembling lips, but it sounded all right to Helene, who was too much wrapt up in the dignity of her new position to have much time to notice other people. She was dressed with extravagant richness; and as everything had been provided for her, and little left to her own taste, she wore nothing that was objectionable in point of material or colour; but the elegance of her attire only seemed to make the coarseness of her style and appearance the more apparent.

"Oh! it don't signify at all," she said, in answer to Elfrida's apology. "We was out all that day, shopping at Southampton. I dare say you think it queer I should want to buy anything, when I'm just come from Paris, but it's things for Ariscedwyn that grandpa wants—tablecloths and such like things. So Mrs. Treherne, and Agnes, and me went together. George wouldn't go, he hates shopping. I don't know what he did with himself all day—moped, didn't you, George?"

"Likely enough," he answered, shortly.

"Ah! I was sure you would. I told you, you wouldn't be able to get on without me."

"Did you like Paris?" asked Elfrida, to stop the exchange of connubialities.

"Lor, yes! pretty well; only it was dreadfully cold there, and they have such little fires. I liked it at first, but it was stupid afterwards. George was so

much out, and he was ill once, and then I *had* a stupid time of it!"

"Have you been ill?" demanded Elfrida, forgetting herself, in a tender anxiety, as she turned to George.

"HI? no, nothing to speak of. What are you talking about, Helene? Why can't you speak of something pleasant, instead of bringing up old things that have happened ages ago? I was a little seedy at one time, but I'm right enough now."

"Oh! you were worse than 'seedy,' George, now," said Helene, pouting, "because you had fever, the doctor said so; and one night you talked all kinds of nonsense, and asked me to come along with you out of England, and" Oh!" said Elfrida, suddenly rising from her seat, "isn't this room insufferably hot? Mrs. Treherne, don't you feel the fire too much? I think I had better set the door open." And suiting the action to

Vol. in. G the word, she drew in a long breath of the fresh cool air from the hall, before she could venture to enter again upon the conversation.

"Do you stay here long *T* was her next question, as she again seated herself by the bride.

"No, we go to Ariscedwyn on Friday. Grandpa's quite vexed at our staying here on our way, but, as I tell him, one can be married but once; unless, indeed, one's a widow, and then perhaps one would think of it a second time. What do you think, Mrs. Treherne? Is once enough for anybody? You've been married longest, and so you ought to know best."

"I think once is quite enough till your first husband's dead," said Elfrida, smiling in spite of herself. She had answered innocently enough, to the silly question asked her; but directly the words were said, she wished she could have recalled them. She thought *he* might think they were intended to bear a double meaning. But if he did, he made no comment: he only said—

"Well, Helene, I'm not dead yet; so I think you had better leave the knotty question till I am. Then, perhaps, you and Mrs. Treherne will be able to settle it satisfactorily between yourselves."

It was cruel of him. She could have cried to him in that moment to spare her, and not speak of such a thing; but his "wife" was present, and she was silent. When Helene rose at last to take her leave, it was with a great assumption of patronising dignity that she feared she should not see Elfrida again.

"We go the day after to-morrow, my dear, and, of course, in my present position, I have such a many calls on my time, that I can't quite say what I can do, and what I can't. George, do you think we shall be able to see Mrs. William again, before we go?"

"I hardly hope so," was his grave answer; "perhaps you had better say good-bye, Helene, at once. You have promised to see so many people, and go to so many places."

"Ah! well, that's just what I said. Well, my dear Mrs. William, I must say good-bye, then, though I'm sorry to part; but I hope you'll come to see us at Ariscedwyn, and make a long stay, for it will be awfully dull there, I expect."

In her pride in being married—and to George Treherne—Helene seemed to have forgotten her old animosity against Elfrida; but her apparent friendliness, like her regrets, was only surface deep, and would not have stood the test of a single rebuff. As she stood there, looking overwhelmingly big in her ample robes and wrappings, her wrists covered with jewellery, her coarse complexion gaining nothing from the contact of delicately-tinted Parisian blossoms, and pale-coloured crepe, she formed a striking contrast to the slight, plainly-dressed figure beside her, whose cold hand she held in her own well-covered palm. The servant had entered some little time before, and lighted the gas, and as the two women stood together beneath the glittering chandelier, the man, whose fate they were, stood by and compared them in his heart—compared the woman he loved, whose beauty he had seen gradually fade, beneath her struggle with her love for him, whose heart he felt now he had wrung far more than God would have wrung it, by his hasty and ill-timed marriage, whose path of duty he had rendered so hard

and miserable by his want of sympathy in her efforts to do right— compared her to the woman he had sworn to love, and honour, and cherish, till death did them part. What wonder if a sigh that might have rent his heart burst from him, as he seated himself by his wife's side, in the carriage which had brought them there, and gave the order to drive " home!" CHAPTER V.

OVEB.

The next afternoon—the last afternoon that he had to spend in Milborough—found George Treherne at the barracks, in his friend Digby's quarters. The last few months had not seen much advance in the suit of this gentleman with Agnes Treherne; still it had not retrograded, and, on his return from the Continent, Agnes had told her brother—her eyes sparkling with anticipated hope—that she really thought "Mamma was coming round by degrees." Charles Digby himself confessed to the miracle of having been bowed to, by Mrs. Henry Treherne, on two separate occasions, when he had met her alone; but she still maintained silence on the subject before Agnes, and constantly spoke of her future prospects as if she did not at all recognize the fact of her engagement. Still, she was less bitter than she had been, and had dropped the habit of introducing the name of Digby only as a pretext for saying something to hurt her daughter's feelings.

The fact is, Mrs. Treherne's temper had been considerably sweetened of late by the fact of her son's marriage with the heiress. The loss of the estate, which he had sustained by the appearance of Helene du Broissart, had been a bitter pill for her to swallow; but knowing his fastidious notions with respect to women, it had never entered her head that the loss could be repaired by his marriage to his cousin. When therefore the announcement had been made to her, that he had proposed in that quarter, and been accepted, her joyful surprise knew no bounds; for George was her idol, and his aggrandizement in this world was all she thought or dreamt of. Before this epoch, the name of the unfortunate heiress had never been men-

tioned, without receiving all manner of abuse at Mrs. Treherne's hands, merited or not; but, directly there was a prospect of her becoming her daughter-in-law, she rose immediately ten per cent. in her estimation, and became as charming, and handsome, and amiable, in the widow's eyes as she had before been ill-mannered, ill-tempered, and plain. Mrs. Treherne had never been wanting in affection to her son, but with his marriage she became more demonstrative than she had ever been before; and scarcely anything engrossed her thoughts, from morning till night, but the newly-married pair. Satisfied on this point, perhaps the prospects of her daughter became less a matter of importance in her eyes, or she thought that, as George was so well married, and master of Ariscedwyn, Agnes being Mrs. Digby, or Mrs. Anybody else, might prove the means of her taking up her abode permanently with her son. Anyway the lancer's suit appeared in a more prosperous way than it had ever done before, and Charles Digby was proportionately elated.

"I declare, my dear fellow," he said to George on the afternoon in question, his honest, kindly face beaming with smiles, "I shouldn't be surprised any day, if I was to get an invitation to dinner at Sorel Cottage. I told you it would all come right in the end, Treherne; you'll see there won't be so much difference in the ages of our eldest sons after all." And Digby ran over with mirth at the idea. But his friend did not laugh with him.

"I don't know whether I ought to congratulate you or not, Digby, on the change; there's no life like a bachelor's, after all."

Charles' blue eyes opened wide with astonishment. ' Well, that's a pretty confession for a married man of three months' standing. What's given you the Hues, George? You don't mean to tell me that you draw any comparison between yourself, as owner of Ariscedwyn, and a poor fellow like me, with nothing before me but a life of slavery?"

"A life of slavery!" exclaimed George Treherne, his eyes sparkling as he spoke; "a life of freedom, you mean;

there's no slavery like being for ever obliged to give in to another's will, as I have to my uncle's. That's what *I* call slavery. Oh! Charges, you can't think what I would give, to be back in the old 120th!" And his eyes fell upon the ground and his hand went up to his head as he spoke. Charles Digby tried to comfort him after the manner of men-comforters. He struck him on the back three or four times, and cleared his own throat and said, "Come, old boy, what's the good of crying over spilt milk? It's a great deal better as it is. There's not a fellow of ours, that wouldn't be deuced glad to change with you," and so on.

It was just as well for George's dignity, that his comfort was administered to him after this fashion. If there had been a woman there, to slip her soft clinging hand into his, and to whisper to him in her tender voice, whilst she knelt by his side, he would have broken down altogether. As it was, he roused himself almost immediately, and said—

"Look here, Charles; you'll come down, and see us as soon as the shooting begins. I don't ask you before, because the country is so dull, but I must have you, and the Colonel, and Fairfax, by the 1st of September. That's a bargain, isn't it?"

"Of course," said Digby, "and only too glad to accept the invitation, George. The covers looked very tempting when I was in Wales in January, but I only got a couple of days' shooting after you went. You have a splendid preserve of pheasants there. I can imagine what pride you'll take in them, old boy!"

"Oh, yes, they are all very well," replied Treherne, indifferently; "but my uncle has plenty of gamekeepers to take all the work off one's hands, and somehow, I don't think one ever enjoys anything half so much when it comes ready-made to you. Do you remember the little box we took together in Dumfries, the year before last, Digby? *That* was enjoyment, if you like. What days we used to have upon the moors! I shall often think of them."

"They may come over again," said Digby, cheerfully.

"Oh, no, they never will. That was

when we were jolly bachelors. Digby, look twice before you leap. There are some constitutions that a married life does not suit."

"Are you well, Treherne?" demanded Digby, becoming quite vexed at his friend's want of spirits.

"Well! yes, never was jollier in my life. What made you ask, Digby? Because of my remark? Oh! I didn't say I was a specimen, did I? I've got nothing to do henceforward, but sit about at Ariscedwyn, and get fat. I shouldn't wonder if I began to take an interest in fattening pigs, or stock, for lack of wholesome employment. You'll find me hard at it, Digby, when you come down, and quite learned in the mysteries of chines, and quarters, and silver-sides, and rounds. Well, I must be going, for we've a dinner party at the cottage to-night, and my lady mother will bring the walls about my ears, if I am not in time, to hand some dean's, or canon's fat wife in to dinner. God bless you, Digby! We shall meet in September."

It was a most unusually serious farewell to come from the lips of George Treherne to another man, and Charles Digby almost started as he heard it. But as he took his friend's offered hand, and seemed to notice, for the first time, what a look of care there lay about his mouth and eyes, his lips re-echoed the blessing he had uttered. And when Treherne had left the room, Digby took his seat at the window, and watched his figure, till it had traversed the length of the barrack-yard, and was about to leave it. Then a sympathetic feeling that he was watched, made George turn round, and wave his stick at his friend before he finally turned the corner, and was lost to view.

"Dear George!" said Digby to himself, with almost a woman's fervour; "Agnes was right in her first conjecture. That marriage will never be a happy one. How could it?"

In the meanwhile George was taking his way towards the Lawn. Only six o'clock, he argued, and the dinner was not till seven. He could walk there and back in half an hour, and then there would be ample time for dressing. He

had no intention of going in; "Of course not," as he said to himself; but he must look at the house once more. He might never see it again. The interview with Elfrida of the day before had upset him completely. Until then, he had been persuading himself that he had been doing rather a fine thing, in sacrificing himself by marrying his cousin. He had fulfilled the wishes of his uncle (his second father) and of his mother, and (since Elfrida wished to renounce even his friendship) done the best thing that he possibly could, for himself, and for her. But the sight of her griefstricken face, the nervous tones of her voice, had upset all his theories, and made him acknowledge what he had known all along, but would not acknowledge—that he had given her the worst possible proof, of the love he had professed to have for her, and had perjured himself in her eyes, as he had in his own. He had tried all he could to lead her wrong; but her good angel had been too much for him, and he had revenged himself upon her virtue by trying to break her heart. As he walked rapidly to the place of his destination, thinking as he went, his conduct appeared more and more despicable in his own sight, till he almost wished he had taken his life before he had married Helene du Broissart. And it could never be undone—never. He had wrecked his own happiness and hers, for life. He was thinking so deeply that he hardly knew where he was, till he came right upon the gates which formed the entrance to the Lawn drive. They were barred gates, and he leant against them thoughtfully, and stared upwards at the various windows of the rooms where he had been so happy. As he gazed, a footstep sounded along the gravel; and before he could move, Elfrida's figure came slowly round the clump of rhododendrons which had hid her from him until then, and looking up, she recognised him at once, and spoke his name. There was no retreating then. He was obliged to enter the gate, and falter out some apology for being there. They both looked sadly conscious.

"I happened to be passing," observed George Treherne, "and stopped to see how the old house looked; but I didn't expect to see you."

"I had been out for a drive," said Elfrida, nervously, "and it was so chilly, I thought I would walk up and down the garden a little, to warm myself," and then stopped.

"It is very cold for May," said Captain Treherne.

"Yes, very; but we have had a long winter."

He had come inside the garden now, and began to pace up and down by her side. "I dare say we shall have all the warmer summer, though, for it," he replied.

"Yes, I daresay we shall," said Elfrida. "How the trees are coming out in leafl" he observed. "The country begins to look quite green."

"Yes; I saw the lilacs were beautiful at Sorel Cottage the other day: we have none here."

"Why, won't they grow?"

"I don't know."

Elfrida's agitation was increasing every minute. She felt as if she could hardly form her syllables. There was a silence between them now, which was more painful than words. George kept twitching off the buds, and tender leaves about him, with his cane as he walked; but he did not speak again. Then he suddenly pulled out his watch, and said—

"By Jove! it's half-past six. I must go. I have an appointment. Good-bye," and he looked wistfully in Elfrida's face as he took her hand. But she only trembled, and faintly murmured "Good-bye" in answer. He held her hand for a minute, warmly, firmly clasped in his, and then turned upon his heel, and left her. But he had hardly done so, when a thought, a mere idea, rushed through her brain; but it was sufficient to make her lose control over herself. What—what if she should never see him again? Elfrida flew down the gravel path, and coming up with him as he reached the gate, she laid her hand upon his arm, whilst her voice shook with agitation.

"George! George!" she said, "you *must* speak to me before you go."

He turned round, startled by her address, but with his face glowing with pleasure at the interruption.

"What is it, Frida?" he demanded.

"Tell me I was right," she said in an imploring voice. "George, say I was right before you go."

"Eight, Frida?" he answered in the tenderest tones. "Yes, I know you were right, in that, as in all things. It is only I who have been wrong."

"Thank God," said the girl, "oh, thank God! I can bear everything now, if you only acknowledge that I was right. You have made my task easy, George. God bless you for it!"

Her simple gratitude almost unmanned him.

"Don't speak to me like that," he urged. "Tell me, Frida, have you forgiven me? *Can* you forgive me?"

"For what?" she asked.

"For this wretched marriage. If I have nearly broken your heart by it, I have quite broken my own."

"Don't say that," she replied. "George, we, must both bear what God sends us. Our paths of duty are plain enough before us now. Heaven help us to walk in them. The very performance of duty may bring happiness at the last."

"Not for me, Frida. I can never be happy with such a wife."

"Hush, hush, dear George! You will come to love her."

"Never! My heart was not made to love twice. I shall meet my wife in Heaven, Frida, but not before."

The girl's face lighted up with almost a holy joy as he spoke.

"In heaven! yes, George. Heaven is always before you. Never forget that. I have led a sinful and a weak life, but I can say to you truly, at this moment, that I would not have it altered if I could. All my sin and weakness and trouble have combined to give me peace. I see now, George, that suffering is necessary to make us look forward to Heaven as our rest. If life could be what we would make it, we should never care to get there. It has all been for the best. Say with me that you believe so."

He could not answer her at first—the man was choking.

"Say you believe it,'George;—that God would not have permitted it, if it had not been for the best."

"I do believe it, Elfrida; but it is you who have made me do so."

"And, George, you will meet me in Heaven! promise me."

Her voice was so earnest in its pleading, as she fixed her tearful eyes upon'him, that he could not but promise.

"Meet you! where would I not go to meet you, Elfrida? Yes, so help me God, if I can."

"He has answered my prayers," said Elfrida, as she gratefully raised her eyes to Heaven. "Go, George, go home to your wife. Life is easy to me now."

So they parted, and it was over.

VOL. III. CHAPTER VI. BETTER THOUGHTS.

Ariscedwyn looked younger and gayer than it had done for many years. The numerous improvements which had been commenced previous to the marriage of its heiress, had been carried to completion during the wedding tour, and old Mr. Treherne, taking greater interest in the place, than he had done since the death of his own sons, was constantly on the move from the house to the stables, the stables to the farm, and the farm to the preserves, to see that all things should be in apple-pie order against the arrival of the newly-married couple. For this marriage had, doubtless, given him the most complete satisfaction. The wish of his heart was fulfilled, at a time when he had given up all hopes of its fulfilment, and the weight which he had carried ever since the appearance of his granddaughter, seemed lifted off his breast at once, and, as he thought, for ever. The prospect of having George to live with him always, and of living, perhaps, to see still younger heir-apparents spring up, to give promise of Ariscedwyn never passing away from the Trehernes, seemed to have taken ten years off the old man's age. During the past year, he had insisted he was too feeble to go about, except upon his pony, or in a carriage; now he might be seen constantly, walking about the adjoining lands and offices, sharply urging the grooms to keep up to their work, and the gamekeepers to have a strict eye to their preserves, that neither the pleasures of hunting or shooting might possess any drawback this year, for Captain Treherne. The fittings-up, and adornments, of the rooms specially designed to the use of the bride, were left by him to female choice and taste; but the gun-room, the billiard-table, and the smoking-room—dedicated to George's heterogeneous collection of pipes and meerschaums—were renovated, and furnished, under his own superintendence, and with the greatest care. It was very evident *which* was the one to whose arrival Mr. Treherne looked forward with such affectionate anxiety. His nephew monopolised every particle of his old heart, and since he had complied with his wishes by marrying Helene, his uncle had become perfectly childish about him. The day that the George Trehernes were expected, he ordered the horses which his nephew preferred to be exercised, in case he should need them on the morrow, as if he was a young, inexperienced rider, to whom a fresh horse implied danger; and on the same morning, he strolled still further—to the gamekeeper's lodge, to see if the kennel was in health, and the young dogs being broken to their work.

"Captain Treherne will be shooting over that pair of Blackboy pups this season, Wyatt; it is time they knew a gun when they see it. You will be sure to break them carefully."

"Never fear that, sir," was the gamekeeper's reply; "but there's plenty of time before us, yet. If I don't deceive myself, sir, there will be work enough for both dogs and guns, this year. It's early days to j udge, but, as far as one *can* judge, there's as pretty a promise of birds as ever I see in Ariscedwyn yet, and that's not saying a little, sir."

Mr. Treherne was delighted with both praise and prophecy.

Ah! well, Wyatt, the Captain will find you plenty of guns, I dare say, and as for game, there can't be too much; we must take care we have no foul work going on, though, as we had last season. Keep the night keepers well up to their work, and if you want extra hands, let me know. Anything to keep the game. How does that rongh-looking fellow, Coles, get on, now? Is he steady?"

"Pretty well, sir, as far as I can judge. He's getting into the ways of the place, and seems to like the life well enough. He cuts up rough occasionally, and is a queer sort of silent fellow at all times, but he works hard and never grumbles."

"That's the principal thing, Wyatt, depend on it. A cheerful willingness always makes a good servant. Never mind his silence; they who talk most often do least. But I mustn't stay longer, for I expect the Captain at home to-day, and I have a great deal to do at the house. Good-morning, Wyatt."

George Treherne and his bride arrived to their time; and old Mr. Treherne experienced such unfeigned delight at receiving them, and was so excited as he followed them from room to room, and heard their expressions of pleasure, and surprise, at the various improvements, that had been made in their absence, that he had no leisure at first to observe any alteration in the looks, or manners, of his nephew. But when the first bustle of their reception was over, and they had settled down into something like order, the change was only too apparent. George Treherne was not the same as he had been. He was very obliging, and ready to comply with others' wishes (particularly his wife's), and willing to join in any plan that might be proposed, but his complete indifference, as to what such plans might be, was evident through it all. Singing, he had quite given up, and his favourite exercise, riding on horseback, he seemed to carry out, only in the most prosaic, matter-of-fact manner. He was more silent than heretofore, and his appetite had considerably failed; but still there were no symptoms of ill-health, nor sufficient evidence of any existing anxiety, to justify his friends in attributing either cause as the reason of the change. Mr. Treherne had noticed it, however, and mentioned it to his nephew; but George had evaded the question, and feigned to laugh at his uncle's concern on the subject. The latter had said one day, that he hoped he wasn't going to have a fever, or anything of that sort.

A fever! The only fever which possessed him, George Treherne knew well enough, was that of Thought—Thought, which had haunted him by night and day ever since he had tried to remedy his first mistake in life by committing the fatal error of a heartless marriage, but never so much as now. Never so much, as since he had seen those imploring eyes raised to his, during that last interview at the drive gates, and heard that tender, pleading voice, asking him to say, to promise, that he would meet her in Heaven! and he had promised, by God's help, so he would! And it was this promise that was burning itself, now into his heart, for George Treherne was a man of his word.? When he betook himself, as (I am afraid to say how many times a day) he did, to his smoking sanctum, there to worship his Nicotian deity, by the offering of a pipe, he would lie back in his easy-chair, whilst he made the atmosphere cloudy, and dense with the volumes of smoke, he slowly, but regularly let loose upon it, and think—generally of Elfrida. Ah! when had he not thought of her, since he had known her? Never—though his thoughts had been varied: first, full of surprise that she had the power to engross and interest him, as no woman had before; then longingly, as whilst toiling along a dusty road we look at some garden full of summer roses, and think how sweet they are, and fresh, and yet never dream of putting forth our hand to pluck them; and then engrossingly, when he knew that she occupied every feeling of his own heart; and then madly, when he asked her to resign her virtue for his sake; and lastly, despairingly, when he flew, with passion and disappointment eating into his life, and married Helene du Broissart. He knew all this; it had passed through his brain, times out of mind—during his daily avocations, on his sleepless bed, even at the very altar, when he had plighted his troth to another woman. From the first moment he had seen her, to the moment he sat in that arm-chair, he had loved her, and her alone! He knew this! But how had he loved her?

That was the question! As the different scenes in the drama of his life, in which she had taken a part, flashed through his mind, he felt she had loved him throughout the same—foolishly perhaps, wrongly certainly, but always *well.* Always seeking his good, his happiness, before her own.

As he sat there, he would review her conduct from the first hour he had seen her, in that very house. How shrinkingly backward she had been, to court his attention, how faithful in her friendship, how loath to acknowledge to her own heart, that she loved him! And when she was forced, by circumstances, not of her seeking, to confess the truth, what horror overtook the poor child, what self-reproach and humility, made her think herself already a degraded creature! And when the great struggle came, between happiness and honour, had Elfrida shrunk from accepting her doom, and renouncing him? And he—how had he repaid her tears, her struggles—struggles for him, as well as herself—her faithful love and friendship? It was this thought, that had drawn the lines of care about George Treherne's face, and made him lose all interest in outward things. "How have I repaid her," he would think to himself, "my love, my dearest r— by giving her the extra pain to bear, of the knowledge of my infidelity, by perjuring myself before Heaven, and her for ever, by injuring two women instead of one. God forgive me!"

Can you wonder if, occupied by thoughts like these, the spirits of George Treherne became inert, and his bodily health failed under the pressure on his mind? Hitherto, he had treated his wife with a great deal of indifference. He seemed to have married her in a sulky, obdurate mood, when he was up in arms with his destiny, and the whole world, and to have revenged himself, by visiting his coldness upon her. He had never been positively unkind to her, but he had been very cold. Fortunately, Helene was not a woman of great delicacy, and did not observe, or, if she observed, think much of, the rough curtness and indifference of his manner; but

strangers had seen it during their brief married life, and made their own remarks upon the subject. But this was changed now. He could not, with that pleading voice, that earnest promise in his ear, do less than Elfrida did. She, a weak and suffering girl, could do her duty, and teach him his; he would, at least, not be backward in learning from her. George Treherne's self-pride came to his aid in this place, and stood him in the stead of virtue. One morning, as he sat smoking in his arm-chair, a great change come over his spirit, a noble resolution took possession of his heart, and thenceforward he arose determined to do his duty, and bear his share of this life's troubles, as a man should bear it.

From that time, his conduct towards his wife changed. His manner was more affectionate, his compliance with her wishes more cheerfully ready, his forbearance with her many moods—from imperious authority, to petulant ill-temper—more genuine and lasting, than it had been. For George Treherne was not a man to do things by halves; he had resolved to buckle on the armour of life, and do battle with himself, and he did it manfully. Hitherto, I have pictured him to you, as a fine, lazy, unprincipled gentleman; that was, because he had experienced no circumstances in his inner life, which should call forth his better feelings, and render him otherwise; but, now that they had come, he proved fully equal to the task he had set himself. Once determined to make the best of the destiny he had chosen—once determined to go in for the right, and maintain it. George Treherne experienced an inward satisfaction, an inward peace, which, reacting on his bodily frame, made both his spirits and his appetite improve. His uncle was delighted at the change, and attributed it entirely to Ariscedwyn air, after a three months' residence on the Continent; "Which was enough," as he said, and believed, "to injure the strongest constitution, if it was only from the messes they put into their cookery." To satisfy his uncle had been easy at all times, but with respect to his wife, I am afraid Captain Treherne found the lesson he had resolved

to master, a harder one than he had anticipated. Unfortunately, Helene was not a woman who could properly appreciate, or make a suitable return, for such an alteration of manner in her husband towards herself. She could not understand it: her conceit made her attribute it entirely to her own powers of fascination, and his inability to stand before them. She was one of those people who require "keeping down." She had behaved pretty well in her married life hitherto, having had a wholesome awe of her husband; but directly his conduct towards her changed, directly he consulted her wishes, and appeared anxious for her opinion or decision, she changed her own conduct with it. From having been tolerably docile, she became imperious in her manner of speaking to him, very boisterous, and, at times, very rude. And had George Treherne not possessed a considerable degree of firmness, he might at this period, have degenerated into that very ugly thing, a hen-pecked husband. But he knew exactly now far to let her go; and when she was almost beyond bounds, and he felt it was necessary to pull her up, the reining-in was so gentle, the curb, if used at all, was so lightly, so dexterously applied, that Mr. Treherne used often to view his forbearance with the greatest surprise, and could scarcely believe this was the same impetuous, self-willed, spoilt little nephew, who used to turn Ariscedwyn upside down with the exhibition of his tempers, some few years since. And neither was it the same! George Treherne was no more the same man he had been a few months before, than Elfrida was the same woman. Their mutual sufferings—their mutual errors—were working a mutual change. The only difference was' that on her the lesson had taken effect sooner than on him. She was gentler, weaker, more submissive and ready to learn; but the end was the same for both. The subject of the William Trehernes, the Lawn, and indeed of Milborough altogether, was, as you may suppose, as far as Captain Treherne was concerned, a closed one. And yet it was often brought suddenly, and directly before him, and gave him occasion for the exercise of all his self-control. Mr. Treherne was very fond of talking of his absent connections, and making all the inquiries he could, relating to them, of his nephew.

"I wish, George," he said one day to him, "that we could persuade Elfrida and William, to come down here for a few months, the change would do her good, as she has not been well, and I think a lady's society would be such a nice thing for Helene, don't you?"

This remark was made upon the doorstep one morning, as they were waiting, with their horses, until Helene should make her appearance for her usual ride, and after there had been an unusually disagreeable display of temper, upon her part, towards her husband. Mr. Treherne did not observe the cloud which came over his nephew's face at his proposal, and waited for an answer to his question, but, "I don't think they would come," was all that George said in return.

"Why not?" asked his uncle. "William is an idle man, and I am sure poor little Frida can't have much to occupy her, as she has lost her baby. I think it would be such a nice change for them both. I shall write and propose it to William."

"We are very comfortable here, sir, alone. Don't you think strangers will break up our family party considerably?"

Mr. Treherne looked at his nephew in surprise. "Strangers," he said, "your own cousins? Why, George, you are not usually so unsociable—I thought you and Elfrida Treherne were great friends. "

George was a man, but he coloured at the unconscious hit, it came so very near.

"So we are, sir—very good friends—and so forth, but—I don't think they'll come," he said, suddenly breaking off his sentence, "whether they're asked or not."

"Who wouldn't come?" inquired Helene, who just then appeared in her riding habit. "Who were you speaking of, George?"

"Of the William Trehernes," he an-swered, as he placed her on her horse.

"Wouldn't you like to have Elfrida here, my dear?" said her grandfather, who was now also mounted with the assistance of his nephew, "she would be such nice company for you, whilst George is out, and about."

"Oh! I'm sure I don't care either way," said Helene; "I like her pretty well, and I think it's horribly dull here, with us three all alone. I dare say it would be livelier if she came. Yes, grandpa, do ask her, she was looking, oh so dreadfully thin and white, when we was at Milborough—wasn't she, George? that day we went to see her, when she stood under the gas, with that black hat on, and I said she looked more dead than alive? You remember, George, don't you?" Yes, he remembered.

"Are you well, George?" said his uncle, suddenly. "I *have* a headache," was the tardy admission "but I suppose it would be high treason, to ask to be excused riding with you, to-day."

"What nonsense! I think it would be very foolish of you to go," answered Mr. Treherne; "the sun is exceedingly hot, and I can see you are not fit for it. Helene and I will ride alone."

But Helene had made up her mind that her husband was going too, and she had no idea of being disappointed.

"How excessively provoking!" she said, without expressing the least concern for his headache, "and when we are mounted, and all. George, I am sure you could come, if you tried: it's all nonsense stopping at home for a headache. The ride will do you good. I do hate to be put out in this way."

He had been so good to her lately, giving in to her wishes in all things, however unreasonable, that she might have spared him for this once; but she was very selfish. Her husband was preparing to comply with her wish, but his uncle stopped him.

"George, you shall not go out in this broiling heat; it's enough, in your state, to give you a fever. Helene, how can you be so selfish? Cannot you see that George is suffering, and when you can ride with him any day too *T*

Captain Treherne did not wish to go.

His head was giving him a great deal of pain, and the sun was very strong; but it was with quite an air of apology that he turned to his wife, and said—

"My headache is really very bad, Helene. Will you do without me for to-day, dear?"

He was standing with his hand on her rein as he spoke, but she twitched it out of his hold.

"Take your hand away, George," she said, with pettish impatience, and without noticing his question. "How can I turn?"

But he still detained her, as he said good-humouredly—

"Come, Helene, give me a kiss before you go."

She stooped her face towards him, her veil drawn tightly over it.

"Not through that thing," he said.

"Oh, then, you can't have it at all," she answered snappishly, "for I can't take the trouble of unpinning it. Come on, grandpa. Don't let us waste all the morning."

"Helene, are you really vexed at my not going?"

"Of course I am," she said, as she'commenced to VOL. III. i set her horse in motion. "I hate to be put out for nothing."

Then he mounted his own horse, and followed her.

"George," exclaimed Mr. Treherne, as he joined them, "you are surely not coming after all *T* "Yes, I am," returned our hero. "You see I can't do without either of you."

He looked towards his wife with a glance of kindness as he spoke; but she had one of her sullen fits upon her, and twice the amount of concession on his part, would not have restored her good-humour until her sullenness had had time to work itself off. He had made the sacrifice to little account, excepting as regarded the inward satisfaction that it afforded to himself.

Mr. Treherne would not allow the subject of asking the William Trehernes to Ariscedwyn, to drop. He renewed it again that evening, and several evenings afterwards, and began at last to express such surprise at his nephew's want of co-operation in his plans, that George was obliged to pretend to share his wishes, for fear his not doing so, might excite his uncle's suspicion.

"I can trusf. to her," he thought to himself;

"she will know it is none of my doing, and she will never come."

And he was right. Mr. Treherne wrote a most pressing invitation for both William and his wife to go down there, and stay with him for an indefinite period, and William was most anxious that Elfrida should accept it, but she would not. He urged, and coaxed, and entreated, and bullied her, by turns, but all to no effect. She steadfastly refused to go to Ariscedwyn. It was a great trial to her, poor girl, for she had no valid reason to give, for not wishing to accept the invitation, and her steady refusal, ascribed to sheer obstinacy on her part, by her husband, only increased his ill-treatment of her, and was a constant subject of altercation between them. Sometimes, she even thought she must give in, that she could not bear the brunt of his reproaches, and displeasure at her determination, any longer; but whenever she thought it over quietly by herself, she felt that, whatever happened, however much she might have to bear in consequence, that she must not, she *dared* not, swerve from her purpose.

George Treherne might well trust her. She was worthy all trust and confidence; and if he had only known what she went through at this time to maintain his trust in her unshaken, he would have honoured her still more than he did.

But those first few days of doing their duty—when the battle was hottest, and victory was as yet an undetermined thing—were weary days both for the truster and the trusted.

CHAPTER VII. THE OATH PUT INTO EXECUTION.

The winter had not been severe, but it had been very long; one of those prolonged seasons which we begin at last to believe will never break—when snowdrops do not appear until April, and lilacs and laburnums blossom with roses in June, and seeds put into the ground

at the usual time, never appear at all, but are frozen to death in their cradles. At such seasons, spring-time is missed altogether, and summer, in its turn, shifts out of place, and we have mignonette blooming in October, and heliotropes and geraniums, making the gardens gay, until the first November frost kills them, when winter sets in, sharp and short, and pulls us all into place again. But after such seasons, the summer heat is very trying. Preceded by no spring days, worthy to be called spring, they appear doubly enervating, from the contrast of the cold of the week before. Nature always seems anxious at such times, to make up for her loss, by being in a hurry. So it had been during the day I am writing of. April and May had been remarkably cold and wintry, but June had come in with a sun worthy of August, and all vegetable life answered to her call. Flowers, which had been embryo buds last week, were opening upon every side, trees seemed suddenly to swell, and expand beneath the heat, until not a crevice was to be detected between their leafy clusters, whilst the air was alive with new-born butterflies, and bees roused from their winter's apathy by the scent of honey. It was not surprising that an old man like Mr. Treherne should feel such a sudden change. The unusual excitement which he had experienced on the return of his nephew to Ariscedwyn was past, and with it the unusual strength he bad for a while experienced, lie drooped as the warm weather set in, and lost his appetite, and was less inclined for exertion than he had been. But no one was alarmed, or even surprised, at the effect it had upon him, because it was only natural. A few months before, his inability to see after his own affairs, would probably have been followed, as he once complained before to George, by neglect of work on the part of his servants and « keepers, and consequent loss to himself. But it was not permitted to be so now. The supervision of the owner of the estate was not only not missed, it was ably, and well supplied, by a younger head, and clearer eyes, than his own. For with those better feelings, which I have de-

scribed George Treherne to have experienced, in my last chapter, had come the desire, without which, but half their work could have been done, to arouse himself from the apathetic, languid state in which he had hitherto spent his married life, and to make himself of some use in his generation. It is the desire which must come to every one of us, sooner or later, who have heads to understand or hearts to feel, the meaning of that short word "*life.*" Perhaps, at first, he did not take a greater interest in the farming occupations, or the stable menage, than he had done before; but with the resolution either to do so, or to do the work without it, the interest came.

Little by little, George Treherne found that the effort to shake off his own thoughts, and to fix his attention on what was going on before him, became easier, until he really liked his work, became interested in the people he employed, and used to be as eager over his discussions with his uncle as to the advisability of that, or the feasibility of this, as he had formerly, been indifferent, to everything that went on at Ariscedwyn. The opinions on the marked change in their young master's conduct, were various amongst his servants. Some thought that it would be time enough, when old Master was gone, for the Captain to take the reins so completely in his own hands; but others—and amongst them was Wyatt, the gamekeeper—said, and truly, that it was a very good thing that the Captain,"who had never been used to work, should turn to it with such a will, and they'd no more have thought it of him, twelve months before, no! no more than nothing!" As for the Captain himself, he cared little, for what any one might say of him, or his proceedings. He had made up his mind as to what was right for him to do, and lie would do it. There is an old proverb to the effect that "the greater the sinner, the greater the saint," which sounds on first reading, as if it was intended for sarcasm. But it is only true. The very determination of will, which leads a man, whose heart has not been directed to better things, persistently wrong, will lead him as persistently in the other direction when his eyes are opened. George Treherne was no weathercock. He had slumbered long—dangerously long—but once roused, you will not find him asleep at his post again. It was one of the bright mornings I have spoken of, and at the gamekeeper's cottage stood, as usual, his daughter Bessie, though she had no occasion this time, to shield her pretty face from the warm June air.

"Have you seen Coles, Bessie?" demanded her father, who had been cleaning his guns, in some of the out-offices.

"Lor, no, father!" answered the girl. "Why, you're always asking after that Coles! I haven't seen him this morning, and I'm sure I don't wish to, either, ill-mannered fellow! I wish he'd take his long face away from the lodge altogether, I'm tired of seeing it!"

"Tut, tut, girl," said the father, smiling whilst he found fault, "you're a saucy lass, and have been spoilt altogether. What has poor Coles done to you, that you should speak against him? Not taken any notice of your pretty face, eh?'

The girl tossed her head disdainfully. "Notice of me indeed, I should like to see him try it, father! Why only yesterday, as I was coming home from the village, through the back covers, I heard a voice muttering, and mumbling, and it frightened me at first, till I saw Master Coles, lying in a trench on his stomach, with his gun in his hand. There he was, pointing it in the air, and talking to himself. Lucky he didn't take me for a poacher, or I should have got shot to a certainty. As it was, I gave him good-morning as I passed, but the rude creature never so much as returned it. Catch me giving my Lord Coles good-morning again, father, that's all!"

The gamekeeper laughed at his daughter's recital.

"Take no notice of a woman, and she'll never forgive you, Bessie. If Coles stays here till his hair is grey, you won't forget yesterday forenoon. Well, well, lass, take your own way, he can bide without your favour, I dare say."

But when the gamekeeper found himself alone, he soliloquised—

"With his gun pointed, and on full cock, perhaps; that's folly. What can the fellow be about? He might have an accident; if he wants practice, he can get it at proper times, and places. I must speak to him about it."

And soon after, as the man Coles made his appearance, he put his resolution into effect. Touching the underkeeper's gun, he said—

"I suppose, Coles, you don't carry this piece on full cock, do you? because it's a custom I don't encourage. Better shots than yourself have repented it before now."

"No, I don't," was the answer.

"And you're careful to keep the cocks well oiled and ready for play? We haven't much use for them just now, but I expect the night-work will begin very soon; for them sneaking poachers ain't over particular, they'd take a sucking leveret, sooner than none, and birds just free from the shell. But they shan't get any of my game *this* year, not if I never get a night's rest, between this, and September. When a bird's brought down by a shot like our young Captain, I call it a glorious death for a dumb creature to die, but to be snared by one of them cowardly night-thieves, why, 'tisn't a fit end even for a brute. But our guns won't do their duty in time of need, if we don't see to them day by day, Coles; it's too late to begin that, after they've missed fire."

"Mine won't miss fire, never fear," said the man he addressed, in a sullen tone.

"Well, 'fore-warned is fore-armed,' as I've often heard old Master say," answered Wyatt, cheerfully, for he was a good-natured man, who took his under-strapper's curtness very quietly. "The Captain's orders yesterday was, that he was going over the kennels this morning, but he didn't send word at what hour. Will you step up, Coles, to the house, and ask, with my duty, what time the Captain wishes to see the dogs?"

"All right," was the answer, as Coles commenced to move slowly away.

"Don't you be long now," shouted Wyatt after him, as he entered the park-gates; btit the words did not seem to have the effect of accelerating the new under-keeper's footsteps. The pace at which he walked was very slow and deliberate, and he seemed to be cogitating deeply, as he sauntered along the park-road, with his eyes fixed upon the ground.

"Suppose I should see her," he thought to himself; "she's been back a month, and I've taken care never to come across her yet; but if I should, would she know me? I think not!"

Scarcely, unless her eyes were brought to bear upon him for long; for he was greatly changed. The long untidy hair was carefully cut, and kept, and a large moustache covered his mouth, whilst new and respectable clothes made an immense alteration in his appearance. But with all his improved outward bearing, there was still the demon lurking in his eye which was there, when last we saw him. He had struggled hard with his passion for drink, since he had been at Ariscedwyn. The man had a fixed and settled purpose in his heart, and he knew he must keep his situation at all risks; But he still indulged to a fatal extent, though less frequently than before. Wyatt had observed the failing in him, but had attributed his melancholy to his desire to overcome it, and had, in consequence, resolved to bear with him and it, as long as it did not interfere with his employer's interests. But there was a still fiercer demon than drink, taking possession of the underkeeper's brain, and every now and then, a wild glance of his eye, startling in its undisciplined glare, would pass like a flash of electricity over his face, and be gone.

"I mustn't meet her," he muttered; "not now, or I might betray myself, and spoil the trick. No, not yet; but when I do, when the time has come"—he ground his teeth together as he spoke— " she shall know if I can *remember* or not." » But he showed none of this disposition up at the servants' hall. He gave his chief's message with the greatest calmness, and received his answer, and then he stayed a moment at the kitchen door, chatting with his informant, who was a pretty pert housemaid, who had no objection to exchanging a few words with the good-looking Mr. Coles. Presently the conversation turned upon the bride and bridegroom, and he bethought him, to ask what the former was like.

"Well, now," said the pert housemaid, "haven't you seen her yet? I never. What's she like? Like other people, I suppose! Ain't that a good enough answer for you?"

"Not half good enough," he replied. "I want to know if she is as pretty as you are."

The housemaid flashed her eyes, and shook all her ringlets at him before she answered—

"How can I tell, Mr. Coles? You must wait till you've see her, and then come and tell me. Well, in the first place, she ain't a bit like me in any way. She's tall, and stout, and rosy as can be, and looks the picture of 'appiness; and well she may with such an 'usband. Lor! I wish I had *her* luck!"

"Do you?" said the under-keeper quickly, and then added, "You shouldn't never wish to be no one but yourself."

"Oh, lor! go along with you," exclaimed the pretty housemaid, "and don't talk such nonsense. Anyways, I wouldn't be you; so there. Now mind you tell Mr. Wyatt, that the Captain will be along that way, in the course of an hour, and be off with you quick, for I've no more time to stop talking to you here."

"Down in the course of an hour, will he?" thought the under-keeper to himself, as he took her at her word, and commenced his walk back to the lodge. "I must keep out of his way. I don't know how it is, but his face is enough to turn a man's mind, a dozen times in an hour. 'Stout and rosy, and the picture of 'appiness,'" and he turned up the sleeves of his coat as he spoke, and surveyed his own arms, through which the large bones seemed almost working their way. "Well, there don't seem much in the past as troubles *her*, anyway. We'll see what the future will bring her."

When he had delivered the message to Wyatt, he was preparing to leave the vicinity of the lodge, and take his way into the park, but his chief recalled him.

"You bide here, Coles; may be I'll want you with the dogs. Jem's gone down to the farrier's for something."

And so he was compelled to remain.

"I must get used to looking on him," he thought, "and one face don't make any difference to another, only his eyes are so deuced soft, when he speaks to a fellow. I wonder if he looks softer still, when he's speaking to *her* /" And the man's teeth set, as the thought passed through his mind.

At the appointed time, Captain Treherne came; but he was not alone. Long before any forms were apparent, through the rejuvenated trees, a loud voice, and occasional peals of laughter, intimated that he was accompanied by his bride.

"Bless her heart!" exclaimed Wyatt, in a burst of enthusiastic fealty; "if the Captain ain't bringing his lady along with him. Don't like to be separated, bless 'em, I dare say. Well, I think I can remember feeling pretty much the same, when I first married Nancy there; we makes no end on 'em at first. Here, Mother, Bessie, here's the bride coming through the park. I know you'll want to have a look at her."

And Mrs. Wyatt and Bessie, wreathed in smiles and thick with congratulations, were consequently standing at their cottage door, all ready to welcome the newly-married pair as they issued from the park gates. For although Helene had been home a month and more, this was the first time she had made her appearance on foot at the gamekeeper's lodge. She was by far too much of a fine lady, to lower herself, as she considered it, by visiting tenantry, or servants employed on her grandfather's estate. Captain and Mrs. George Treherne did not look like a very loving couple, as they walked. There were no clasping arms to be untwined, no tender pressure to be relaxed, no meeting eyes, to be bent upon the ground, nor even faces turned towards each other, to be quickly occupied with examining the

horizon, as they suddenly came in sight of the strangers.

The husband was walking on one side of the pathway, the expression of his face grave, and subdued, his eyes downcast, his whole demeanour more like that of a man, preoccupied by pressing business, or care, or thought, than that of a bridegroom of three months' standing.

His wife, on the other hand, formed a striking contrast to him. She was elaborately dressed for the time of day, and the rural walk. Her manner was triumphant, boisterously so; her tone of voice confident, and she appeared to be monopolising almost all the conversation. Every now and then, she would be heard apparently asking him a question, now imperatively, then coaxingly, but always loudly, and with VOL. III. K an air of self-importance, generally accompanied by a tap of her parasol, when the answer did not come immediately upon her demand. As the Wyatt family offered their timid congratulations, Helene accepted them, with what she considered a dignified indifference; whilst George (ah! what a mockery those congratulations seemed to him) invariably stopped, to thank his well-wishers for the kindness of their thought, and to express a wish in return, that it might come true. It was angelic in him to do so, for they wearied him to death; and as soon as he decently could, he turned the conversation to the kennel, and expressed his intention of going over it. Then Wyatt discovered that his under-keeper was not forthcoming, and that he must go himself with his young master. He had other business to attend to, and the defection on the part of Coles, annoyed him.

"Very provoking," he thought; "that man must be getting negligent. I am sure I gave the order distinctly enough. I must speak to him about it. Carelessness won't do here."

But had the under-keeper possessed the gift of second-sight, he need not have disappeared at the moment he was most wanted, for Mrs. George Treherne refused to go over the kennel.

"How you can ask me, George, I

can't think," she daintily exclaimed; "why the soles of my boots are like brown paper, and I know that kennel is always wet and dirty. I couldn't, indeed. "

"Never mind, dear," said her husband, goodhumouredly, under the full force of that new resolution he had made, to speak and act to her, always with kindness; "I thought you would have had on thick boots, at this time of the year, and might have liked to see the dogs. But what will you do? I shall be some time here."

"Some time—what, with those horrid animals?"

George smiled. Perhaps it was the idea how much nobler dogs are, than some people, that made him smile.

"Yes, really, Helene, with those 'horrid animals,' as you call them. I have old dogs to renew my acquaintance with, and new dogs to examine, and sick dogs to physic. I dare say I shall be an hour."

"Oh, bother!" exclaimed Helene. "I can't stay about for an hour, George. Why didn't you tell me so before you came?"

"My dear," he answered gravely," it was your own wish to accompany me. My appointment was with the gamekeeper. I will be as quick as I can, if you would like to wait in the lodge."

"No, I can't wait in the lodge," said Helene, her temper rising. "I shall go home, if you like dogs better than me."

She intended this thrust to be very telling, but her husband was too honest to pretend he felt it. But as she turned hastily away in the direction of the park gates, he followed and stopped her.

"Helene," he said, kindly, "I am sorry you came out for nothing. Shall I walk home with you? I can return to the kennel afterwards."

"No!" she answered, pettishly; "I can walk home very well alone," and prepared to pursue her way; but still he demurred.

"Perhaps I had better go with you," he said.

"I *tell* you I don't *want* you," she answered, still more crossly; and the tone struck him, and he ceased to urge the subject.

"In that case," he said, "I will follow you as soon as I can, and we can ride as we agreed, in the afternoon."

He waited where he stood, a pleasant smile of farewell lingering on his lips, in expectation of receiving such a one in return from her, but she never turned her head, and then he walked into the kennel without further comment, but his heart felt chilled and dispirited, as he did so.

She stood for a few moments irresolute, and then she gathered up her silken skirts, and commenced picking her way homewards. For though Summer was on them, she had come too suddenly to dry up and scatter, all at once, the multitudes of dead leaves which the blasts of a colder season had strewn, and the rains had beaten down, upon that shaded pathway through the park, where the sun seldom shone with any degree of fervour. The scene around was a lovely one; but the mere contemplation of its loveliness, had no power to arouse any feelings of pleasure in Helene's breast. Indeed, I doubt, if she even observed that it was beautiful. The songs of the birds, so grateful to Heaven for the sunshine and the promise of plenty, roused no answering chord in her breast. The scent of blossoming hawthorn bushes, the balmy air, so refreshing yet so soft, had no power to exhilarate her spirits, or to lighten her footsteps. As she strolled homewards that morning, she was thinking, not of any of these things, not of the Hand from which they came for her enjoyment, but of the bore it was to have a husband who cared about dogs, and how glad she should be when the pathway was quite clear, and she should not have to pick her way, mingled with a doubt, as to whether it would be worth while to wear her best dresses, whilst she was alone with "grandpa and George," and whether she had better not reserve them for the shooting season, when she had heard that several friends were expected to join them.

She had traversed about half her distance, and was in the centre of the large park, when she suddenly came upon a figure, that appeared strange to her. Suddenly, I say, because the man was lying down, with his face from her, as she approached, and at first he did not move from his position. But Helene had a great idea of finding fault with any trespassers upon the estate: devoid of timidity, and of a haughty disposition, she had often drawn down upon herself hearty curses, and not unfrequently to her face, for the summary style in which she had ejected strangers, at various times from her grandfather's domains. As soon as she caught sight of the figure I have mentioned, she quickened her footsteps, and came angrily upon, what she considered, the intruder. "Man," she exclaimed, "who are you?—what are you doing here? Do you belong to Ariscedwyn?"

The man she addressed rose slowly from his recumbent position, and confronted her. For the moment, she did not recognise him, and repeated her question—

"Who are you? Do you work on the estate?"

Still he looked at her steadfastly, without so much as blinking, and then the colour left her rosy cheeks, and she faltered again, but, this time, with an inkling of the truth—

"Who are you? What do you want?"

"Who *am I*? repeated the man after her, slowly, but with an expression of the profoundest contempt. "Who *am* I? you did ought to know, Nell Willis."

The colour still further forsook her face, and for once in her life, Helene looked really pale.

"*You* here!" she faltered. "For God's sake, *why*? I haven't harmed you, John, what do you want with me?"

"You haven't harmed me?" he answered, looking her full in the face; "haven't harmed me, Nell? Do you come in your silks, and laces, with the marriage ring on your finger, to tell me that? What do you call *not harming ʃ* Telling a fellow you loved him as yourself, and couldn't never marry another, swearing it to him, till he'd have risked his life upon your faith, and then deserting him, and taking a gentleman to your husband? Do you think 1 1 1 stand it? Stand by and see him owning of you, and be quiet? I've followed you for this, Nell, followed you to get an answer to the question I'm asking you. What did I say I'd do to you, if you married, saving it was to me?—answer me that!"

"I forget," she said, almost in tears.

"You forget?" he shouted; "forget what I said to you at Blackheath? Then I'll remind you: I said I'd"

He did not finish his sentence, but, cocking the gun in his hand, pointed it at some imaginary object in the air. The click of the trigger, as it yielded to the pressure of his hand, filled her very soul with horror.

"John," she shrieked, "you wouldn't do that! you don't mean it; you weren't in earnest; tell me, John?"

Perhaps, in all her life, she had never appeared more interesting than she did now; her terror, though it was for herself, lent her a more womanly aspect, in the agitation which it caused, and her words came from her lips with a trembling, faltering accent, which was very foreign to words of hers. He observed it; but it was terror for the consequence of her actions, not grief for the actions themselves, and the sight only hardened him.

"Wasn't I in earnest?" he repeated, with a mocking deliberation: "you'll see, Mrs. Treherne, before long, if-1 was in earnest—I only wait my time You haven't laid on my breast, and met my lips— yes, mine, the navvy's and the under-gamekeeper's, for nothing; you shall pay for your whistle, by God! I used to love you, with every fibre of my heart, but you've turned my love to gall, and I hate you—I hate you now, Nell Willis, as I hate the thought of hell! A life for a life. You've taken mine already— or all that was worth calling' life,' in it." And he commenced playing with the murderous weapon he held in his hand, with a careless indifference as he spoke.

Helene Treherne was blanched with terror, but she summoned up courage to say, "I shall give intelligence of your threats, directly I reach home. Do you think, that you will be permitted to remain on this estate, to insult the mistress

of it? You forget that I am no longer Nell Willis, and this is not Chelton-Marsh. I have friends to protect me here, and"

But before she could finish her sentence he had grasped her arm.

"Hold hard, my lady," he said; "think twice of what you are saying. By heavens! if you utter a word of what I've told you, or even hint, that you've seen me, or who I am, there's not a common varlet thin twenty miles of Ariscedwyn, but shall know that Mra Treherne has had her grandfather's underkeeper for a lover, and stooped to be false to him. They shall know more than that, Nell! They shall hear a better part of the story than that. They shall hear all about a certain 14th of July, and a night at sea. What do you say to the bargain?"

She was breathing hard, and short now, and her colour came and went, by sudden rushes.

"John Bead," she managed to say at last, "you are mad. I'll give you money—love—anything—so you'll hold your tongue, and spare me."

"Ah! you've come to begging, have you?" he sneered. "I thought that would bring you to something like it, but it ain't of no use—money? what's money to me? I've no call for it; and love— would you give me as a bribe, Nell Willis, what's mine by right as a man?"

Then her quick, undisciplined temper got the better of her fear, and she turned round upon him—

"Eight! how dare you talk of right? my love is my own, to give or to take, as I choose."

"But you took mine in exchange, Nell, that wasn't your own, to keep, or to throw away, as you chose. It was better stuff than yours—but you've played fast and loose, with it, till it isn't fit for another woman's service. You've lied to me all along, in saying that you loved me—isn't it the truth, now?" he shouted, rather than said, and then waited for her answer. She was driven into a corner; she knew he wouldn't believe her, even if she denied it again, and so she tried to brave it out.

"Yes, it is the truth," she said. "I never cared for you—not even at Chelton-

Marsh. Now you have it, let me go. I've nothing more to say to you:'' and she prepared to pass him, but he stood across her pathway.

"You *never* cared for me?" he said in a low voice; "*never?*—say that again, Nell Willis."

"Why should I have cared for you?" she answered in a burst of passion, taunting him; "a low vagabond, without money or means, or"

"Wyatt," said George Treherne, as they were leisurely inspecting the various kennels of dogs, "who's firing at this time of the day? I thought I gave orders last week, that the men were never to let off their guns before the evening. It's not safe—if the guns require cleaning, let them draw their charges."

"I don't know, I'm sure, sir, unless it's that fellow Coles. I gave your orders last week, as particular as possible, to all the men; but Coles has certainly become more careless and indifferent, of late, than he used to be—sometimes he appears to me as if he didn't hear."

"He *must* hear, if he wishes to keep his place," rejoined Captain Treherne. "Speak to him again about it, Wyatt, and tell him, at the same time, that I allow nothing like negligence on this estate. Let me see the new litter of Hanger pups, and then, that must do for to-day."

And in the meanwhile, across that damp, and sunless pathway in the park, her bravery of silk, and velvet, and snow-white feathers, contrasting strangely with the heap of dead and sodden leaves, upon which she had fallen, lay the body of Helene Treherne— only her body—her soul had gone, frightened out of its mortal housing, by the cruel bullet and shot of her lover's gun, before the taunting sentence, with which she had intended to greet him, had fully left her lips. Dead, and alone, she lay—her face upon the ground—her arms outstretched before her, just as she had stretched them, in the ghastly agony of death, in the sudden fear of falling. With her last words, true as they were, words of cruelty—with no spark of pity in her bosom, for the man she had driven to madness—with no looks of love to support her—with not a thought of the God who waited to receive her—Helene Treherne passed to the bar of judgment. It was an awful death, but the life which had preceded it, had been more awful still—a life of deceit, of self-love, of worldly ambition, and utter disregard of Heaven. How could the death be too horrible, which should match such a living! And yet she was young, with a prosperous future apparently before her; and it is very sad to think of her, lying in that lonely pathway—her features marred and mangled, by the fatal shot—her chance of reformation—of awakening to a better, truer life, gone for ever. In that hour—if spirits are permitted to have cognisance of the events which agitate this lower world—I wonder if one, whose death was scarcely happier, was hovering near, and reading, in the wretched end of her only child, the consequences long drawn out, and yet to be connected, of the fatal error which led to her desertion of the creature, which God had given her, to train for Himself! If so, she must have felt then, if she had never felt before, that there is no greater need to make a hell, than the reviewing of the consequences of our own sinful actions, when it is past our power to remedy, or to recall them.

For one moment had the unhappy murderer lingered by his victim—for one moment had he stood and gazed, upon the prostrate form of the woman he had so much loved; then, as he watched the ruin he had made—saw the sickly pallor of death, gradually overspread the set features—the violet-tinted shade take possession of the hands, which were grasping the damp ground where they lay—the fitful look which had occasionally appeared in his face, the wild, maniacal glare, which had been seen to dance, and glimmer there, gradually gathered over it again, like a drawn veil, and settled down; and then, with a sudden look of intensest fear at the deed he had done, he sprang away with loud cries from the horrid scene of his work of destruction, leapt through the surrounding thicket, and was gone.

And still she lay, amidst the stillness, and the loneliness of the surrounding scene, the stillest, loneliest thing there; the gun, with which the deed had been accomplished, lying close to her, where the madman had first thrown it down, as the full horror of his action burst upon his bewildered senses. And there she lay, through the best part of that bright June morning—unfound, and alone.

CHAPTER VIII. THE ABREST.

George Teeherne, skirting the park, on his way homewards, in order to visit a pheasant preserve, that lay between the gamekeeper's lodge, and the house, little dreamt of the dreadful tragedy, which had taken place within so short a distance from his footsteps. His immediate business over, his thoughts reverted to the last words he had had with his wife, and thence, to many words and scenes of similar import. Sad thoughts they must have been, for he had hardly known, when he made that resolution to try and win her affections, what a hard thing it is, to live in close and daily contact, with the undisciplined temper of one, who is nearly connected with you. And yet he made excuses for her, to himself, as he strolled homewards that bright June morning, on the score of her parentage, her bringing up, and his own want of love towards her. He would try again, perhaps there had been something defective in his manner of treating her ill-humour—it would be strange, if he could not manage, by hook or by crook, to bring a woman round to love him; and when she loved him, things would go smoother. As the idea flashed through his mind, a particle of the old conceit curled his lip, at the bare notion of his encountering difficulty in the subjugation of a feminine heart. Afterwards, how glad he was to be able to look back, and say truly, that on that morning, no thoughts of her, but kindly ones, had filled his own heart.

On his arrival at the house, and first discovery that Helene was not there, no idea of alarm occurred either to him, or Mr. Treherne. She might very well have come in, and gone out again, without any one seeing her; it was still early—about twelve o'clock; she was probably in the garden, or grounds. But the

luncheon was put on the table, and the groom came round for orders about the horses, and the time of riding, and still Mrs. George Treherne had not made her appearance; and then her husband, fearing that her continued absence, betokened a more than usually lengthy fit of displeasure with himself, commenced a search for her, over the adjoining premises, calling her name as he went, with a view of VOL. III. L s finding, and conciliating her. But in the meanwhile a messenger came to the kitchen premises—a tiny messenger of some six years old, who, with blue eyes starting out of her head, and wide open, trembling mouth, came running from the park, to tell how the lady "was sick there, and had tumbled down." To the eager inquiries from all sides of "where?" the only answer that could be gained was, that it was in the path where "the many primroses had growed." But as the park paths in spring were all masses of primroses, the explanation was not lucid. As it was, however, it proved sufficient to send half a dozen strong men, George Treherne at their head, running like madmen down the park road, whilst they looked on all sides for what they sought. But there were many paths there; and as they diverged from the main road into one of the more sequestered tracks, Stevens, the old butler, who had been years at the hall, laid his hand upon George Treherne's arm, and held him back—

"Not you, sir. Let me go first."

For he had caught a glimpse, already, of a fallen, outstretched figure—fallen as living people do not fall, with violet-tinted hands grasping the damp earth—and he guessed the truth at once. But his master would not be restrained; he, too, had seen the sight before them, and he exclaimed authoritatively—

"Stevens, let me go! No one touches her but myself."

Then the men-servants drew back, appalled and awe-stricken, and the young husband went up alone to that outstretched figure. His first idea was of a fit, or a faint; he had no conception of the truth. Tenderly, he lifted the body—tenderly, turned the face towards himself; and then—they all saw it. There was no more possibility of misconception; the features were fixed in death; the bullet wound, right in the centre of the forehead, had blown that and part of the scalp away. To say that George Treherne was shocked, is saying too little; and yet there is no more to be said. He had not loved this woman; and, therefore, it was not grief, that assailed him at the sight of her lifeless body: it was an awful, almost overwhelming, shock to every nerve he possessed. As the dead face caught his eye, he turned ghastly pale, and trembled so much that he could scarcely support the weight of the corpse. His servants were too horror-struck to speak to him; they only stood apart in silence, and looked at one another. After a few minutes, George Treherne said, in a hollow voice—

"Stevens, who could have done this ?"

But the butler could not even make a guess at the perpetrator of so foul a murder—none of them could. It was all wrapt in the most awful mystery.

When Captain Treherne spoke again, it was almost passionately.

"Stevens," he said," go home at once; tell Robson to take one of the carriage horses, and ride as hard as he can for Sir Henry Griffyths. You, John," he said to another, "go back with the rest, and bring a door, or a hurdle, or anything, and something to cover—to cover—it with."

He could hardly bring himself to speak of her in the neuter, and the word came from his mouth hesitatingly, and almost with tears. But the butler entreated to be allowed to remain.

"You mustn't stay here alone, sir. Pray let me stay with you."

"No, Stevens. I wish you particularly to be at the house, that your master may hear nothing till I can tell him myself. One of you can remain with me, if you like. Let the rest go, and do as I said."

The man who remained gave it afterwards as his evidence, that the Captain never spoke so much as a word, the whole time he was near him, but rested on the bank, with the dead body of his wife in his arms until the other servants returned with a door, which they had taken off its hinges, and a couple of sheets, in which he wrapt and covered the body, and placed it tenderly upon its rough bier. Then the sad cavalcade commenced their slow, measured march homewards. As they came in sight of the house, George Treherne went forwards, and broke the news to his uncle. He did it as gently, as cautiously, as lovingly as he could, but no caution or love could prevent the blow falling on the poor old man's head with stunning violence. There is no other simile, that could so well describe the effect, the intelligence had upon him. He was too old to bear the shock. It had made the young head and body of George Treherne reel; but the grandfather seemed to sink under it at once. It was just, as if you had brought a mallet down upon his head, and stunned him. He could not think, or comprehend, or act. He simply sat down under it, and allowed it to overwhelm him. Before the evening fell, the magistrate of the county, Sir Henry Griffyths, who was an old friend of the family, had arrived, summoned by the messenger which George Treherne had despatched for him. Then questions began to be asked, and inquiries made, as to the probable reason of so foul an act being perpetrated, and so near the house. On the second day, an inquest was held upon the body, at which all the servants appeared, to give such evidence as they might, concerning the probable reasons for the murder. Here the evidence of the keeper, James Wyatt, who affirmed to the mysterious way in which the man, Thomas Coles, had become engaged in the situation he had filled on the estate of Ariscedwyn; of his taciturn habits, his strange wandering manner, and the circumstance related by his daughter Bessie —who was brought forward to tell her own story— of his having been overheard muttering to himself in the park, whilst he pointed his gun to some imaginary object in the air—was considered so conclusively to point suspicion at the man mentioned (particularly as the gun which had been picked up near the body of Mrs. Treherne was recognized as the one used by him), that Sir Henry Griffyths caused a warrant to be issued for the apprehension of one Thomas Coles, and a proper search to be instituted in the surrounding counties for the suspected murderer. And yet no one imagined that it had been a deliberate murder. The general opinion was, that the man had been carelessly playing with his weapon, and, having shot his mistress by accident, had fled in fear and horror at the deed; or that he was mad, and unconscious of what he had done. Any way, he must be arrested. The public indignation, as the story became known, was extreme. It would have been so in the case of any one, gentle or simple, shot down on their own ground, and in broad daylight; but where the subject of the murder was such a one as Helene Treherne, a lady, so young, and lately married, heiress to one of the oldest properties in the county, it knew no bounds. Every one who could do so themselves, or who possessed the means of furthering the search, joined in the hue and cry; and horror at the deed, wonderment at its motive, and lament for the murdered bride, filled every heart and mouth. But whilst they hunted far and wide, and wondered and lamented, the object and cause of their indignation was close to them, if they had only known it. When those horrid cries which burst from the wretched murderer on the completion of his crime, first sounded on the empty stillness of the park glades, he had dashed away with an instinctive desire, mad as he was, to hide himself from view — dashed into the thickest underwood, through tangled briers, and into dells, overgrown with matted creepers, and carpeted with tall grass and stinging-nettles—into the darkest recesses of that grand, wild growth of wood, where, even in the trodden paths, it was easy to lose oneself, and there lay down, panting from the horror which had overtaken him at the deed he had done, and at the sense of nervous dread, which those feel, upon whom insanity is surely creeping. There he lay, through all the first night, and second day, immoveable — silent, except for hoarse whispers which occasionally broke from him, and for that heavy breathing which never ceased.

They never thought of looking for him in the park; they never dreamt, but that he would put as much distance as he could, between himself and the scene of his great crime. And so, while scouts were after him in every direction, he lay there, hidden— unnoticed; and the second day drew to a close, and the second night arrived. How awful the night is when Death is in the house! The day is solemn enough, but the night is worse. When the stillness around us, is almost as profound as the stillness of *that thing,* that lies upon the bed beside us, looking so unnaturally lengthened beneath the sheet which covers it, we could almost cry out to the invisible spirits in the air around us, to appear and speak—anything to break the universal silence. But I am writing of those who watch the dead only, not of those who love and watch them. To such, anything is better—any silence, any gloom, any length of watching—than the idea, that only a few more hours must go by before the form of what they so much loved, lifeless, decaying matter though it be, is taken away, and hidden from their eyes for ever. If they might only keep this senseless body, only be able to look on the dead face of their beloved for always, they could bear the rest. They could bear to have their passionate appeals unanswered, their loving looks unreturned, if they might only be spared the bitter pain of laying this cherished form, in the cold, damp earth. So they say, and think, in their blind, unreasoning folly, not knowing, or rather, not choosing to believe, that God, in His great mercy, has ordained that our nature renders the sacrifice of burying our dead out of our sight necessary, in order to save His creatures from a life-long agony, and give them the chance of having their grief softened, and assuaged, by the influence of time and forgetfulness. But there was no such loving, heart-broken watcher by the bed of Helene Treherne. She lay upon the couch where she had so lately slept, a bride by her husband's side, dead and alone, through the darkness of the night. For her husband was occupied in watching

by his uncle's bedside, who had been taken ill the day before, from the shock he had sustained. Near them was located Sir Henry Griffyths, for as his home was many miles away from Ariscedwyn, it was thought advisable he should stay there for a few days, until news might arrive of the arrest of the murderer. He was further prompted to this act, by the fact of his being an old friend of Mr. Treherne's, and consequently anxious to be near him in his trouble. Rooms had been arranged for him, and the young widower near that of the old man's, and at some distance from the apartment where the dead body lay.

To the servants, had been intrusted the charge of watching the corpse, and the servants, being superstitious, shirked their duty, as such hireling mourners will. The day had been as hot as the preceding one, and the night was close and sultry. The house at Ariscedwyn was too far in the country, for the inmates to be afraid of burglary, and in summer both doors and windows were as often left unfastened, as not. On the night in question, the windows of the room where the body of Helene Treherne lay, were thrown wide open, but there was scarcely sufficient air to stir the white blinds which were drawn over them. The woman who had performed this office, had observed at the time to the trembling housemaid who held the light for her, and who could not be persuaded to advance within the threshold, that "it was mortal bad weather for a corpse, and it didn't seem to make any difference, if the windows were left open or shut." And then the housemaid had recommended her, to draw the blinds up a little, for she had observed, "There's no one to see in, and if there was, what matter?" And so the blinds had been half-way drawn up, and the lamp lighted, without which the lower orders would think it sacrilege to leave the dead; as if the spirit on which the infinite wonders of another existence have burst would care to revisit this earth, to inspect its remains by the aid of wax candles, or a few half-pennyworths of gas! But whilst we are mortal, we shall never learn to regard a dead body

as it is—the cast-off clothing of an enfranchised spirit; the worthless remains upon which perhaps one of God's angels is already looking with contempt— "The proud contempt of spirits risen," as Mrs. Barrett Browning has it, in one of the last pieces which issued from her pen. And so the servants, although they were afraid to stay in the room with Death, reverentially lighted the lamp, before they closed the door, and left Helene Treherne to her unwaking sleep, and retired to sit up (in company with some others, for the sake of their nerves) in the housekeeper's room, where they indulged in many hot potations, (also, for the sake of their nerves), and related various horrible ghostly tales of walking corpses, and people buried alive, and such like cheerful subjects; until they excited each other's fears to such an extent that they were almost afraid to sit up, even in company, and would have been still more so, to go to bed. But whilst they sat and talked, huddling together, warm as the night was, for very dread of feeling themselves alone, a sound fell on their ears. Large as the house was, the utter stillness which pervaded it, rendered a very slight noise perceptible, and this noise was not slight. They listened at first, breathlessly, almost disbelieving their own senses; then, as the disturbance became distinct, and the quarter from which it proceeded more decided, they gathered, a trembling group, in the passage, every hair on their heads standing on end.

"It's never," cried the old butler Stevens, every pore breaking out with perspiration as he listened, "it's never from the Blue-room, Mrs. Watson?"

The Blue-room was where the corpse lay. The same room, which had been freshly adorned and furnished, for the reception of the bride and bridegroom, so short a time before.

"It is then, Mr. Stevens, it is from the Blue-room —it's the mistress as has risen again. Mercy on us! what shall we do ⸮ A cold shiver ran through the little group, and a scream burst from one of the maids.

"Don't you do that, Hannah," exclaimed the housekeeper, scarcely able to bring out her words, "or you'll bring it down upon us. Oh! Mr. Stevens, what can it be?"

They listened again, advancing a little further along the passage, and now there could be heard distinctly the tread of footsteps about the Blue-room, and the tones of a voice, sometimes raised as in anger, sometimes low and wailing.

"It's my belief," said Stevens, presently, "that it's the corpse, as is about to point out its murderer. I've heard of such things before. Murder will out."

"What are we to do?" asked a young footman, braver than the rest; "we can't stop here doing nothing;" whilst the women were crying with their fear, and shaking all over.

"Let us go and call the Captain and Sir Henry," said the butler.

"Oh! don't.leave us here," shrieked Mrs. Watson. "Me and Hannah, we must come with you, Mr. Stevens. We shall die if you leave us by ourselves."

The noise had increased greatly during the conversation, the footsteps could be heard rapidly pacing the room, and the voice was loud and violent. Kendered desperate by their fears, the group of servants now advanced along the passage, and up the corridor, where the rest of the household slept. They had to pass the dreaded Blue-room on their way; but anything was better than their suspense. As they approached it, the disturbance within was so plainly distinguishable, that, with a general exclamation of horror, they ran past the door, and gained the passage, which led to the part of the house where Mr. Treherne usually slept, and which was much detached. The old man was not asleep, but lying on his bed immoveable, wrapt up and absorbed in his own thoughts, his nephew dressed, and watching by his side, when the affrighted group knocked at his door, and, as soon as they could gain admittance, burst into his room, with the astounding intelligence that the body of Mrs. Treherne was walking about the house, and talking. The news, incredible as it was, roused Mr. Treherne from his apathy; all the entreaties

of his nephew, who was very much disposed to swear, at what he considered the servants' superstitious folly, could not persuade him to stay in his bed. He got up, put on his dressing-gown, and insisted upon going to the Blue-room himself, accompanied by George and Sir Henry Griffyths, who had been also awakened by the general alarm. His friend wished as much to dissuade him from his design, as George had done, for he had not yet seen the corpse of his granddaughter, and he feared the effect, the sight might have upon him. As to the story of the footsteps and the voice, George Treherne and Sir Henry Griffyths were perfectly contemptuous on the subject, and regarded it as a mere chimera, born of fear, on the part of the servants. But old Mr. Treherne insisted upon having his own way, and as the party proceeded towards the room where the corpse lay, the sounds, of which the domestics had complained, became distinctly heard by them all. The women commenced screaming again, but the men, with George Treherne and Sir Henry Griffyths at their head, immediately pressed forward, and merely saying, "Sir Henry, some one must have broken into the room, who has no business there," George Treherne turned the key and handle of the door almost simultaneously, and throwing it open, rushed into the apartment, followed by the rest. As they entered, the first thing that they noticed was that the corpse had been uncovered, and the bandage which had been placed around the forehead, to hide the mutilation caused by the gunshot wound, withdrawn. At the foot of the bed, leant the figure of a young man, dressed in untidy, weather-stained clothes, with a disordered mien and matted hair, with a wild look in his eye, and a seemingly total unconsciousness of the presence of the party before him, which too surely betokened the state of his intellect. As the men-servants caught sight of him, they exclaimed, with one voice, "Coles!" and George Treherne was about to rush forward and seize him, but Sir Henry Griffyths laid his hand upon his arm, and with difficulty re-

strained him. The man was gesticulating violently, as the door was opened, and he did not cease for one moment, or appear to notice that he was interrupted. "I wouldn't have

A killed you," he exclaimed, addressing the corpse with a pathos that was most touching to listen to, —" I wouldn't have hurt a hair of your head, if you'd only been true to me, even though they made you marry another man; if you'd only have told me, Nell, that all our days of love weren't quite forgotten, nor likely to be; if you'd only have said, as you remembered Chelton-Marsh, and your heart was sorry for'the pain mine suffered in our separation. But you taunted me, and threw my breeding in my teeth—I, who would have died for you; I, who loved you so dearly, and who you used to say, Nell, that you loved as well. Oh! forgive me, Nell, you and the devil tempted me to it. Speak, and say you forgive me for it now! Say you'll love me, when we meet again, and I'll shoot myself, and come after you!",

Then the wretched man proceeded to lay his hands again upon the corpse, but the sight was too much for the outraged husband of the murdered woman. He had been standing quietly till then, kept back by the whispered entreaties of his friends, but neither these, nor their manual force, could restrain him any longer. His face had changed, as he listened to the words of the madman before them, his nostrils VOL. III. M had dilated, and his breathing become short and heavy, as he heard his tones of tenderness in addressing the dead body. As the speech was concluded, he would be quiet no longer. With one shout and bound, he sprang forward, and threw himself upon him. The man, taken by surprise, permitted his antagonist for one moment, to be the master, but directly he understood that the intentions were not friendly, he turned, and grappled with him. The muscular, sinewy grasp of John Eead, would at any time have been fearful odds, for the tall, slender frame of George Treherne to contend against, albeit the latter was well and athletically made; but he had not had the work to develop his muscles, that the other had, added to which, he had now to struggle with the unnatural strength of a madman. But there was a sudden strength in George Treherne that moment, born of a great and dreadful fear, which was almost as unnatural, as the strength developed, by frenzy. The fear, that his name, and the honour of his dead wife would be compromised before his own domestics, if the murderer's revelations were not stopped, lent him a force he had not believed himself capable of. He seemed to be straggling, rot with powers of flesh and blood, but with something which, if not subdued and silenced, would blight the whole of his future, as his past had been blighted. For to those present, who knew the previous history of Helene Treherne, and whose minds were enabled, by the development of education, to take in at once, the meaning of the wretched man's address, and connect it with the mysterious murder and the unfortunate woman's past life, his words had not required much more explanation. They seemed to comprehend the whole misery of the story at once, and it was no longer a mystery to them. It was a fearful scene; the stillness of that death chamber, which should have been holy, broken by the stamping of feet, the noise of blows, the occasional shout of an oath, as the two men wrestled together, by the side of the dead body of the woman who had been the curse of them both, and yet for whom they were equally ready to fight. George Treherne grappled with his rival as if he intended to kill him on the spot, as, indeed, he said he would.

"George," exclaimed his uncle, "for God's sake give over I remember where you are—in the presence of her dead body."

"It is because I remember where I am," he shouted in reply, as he prepared to close again with the madman, "that I will not give over. Do yon think I will let this brute slander my wife's name, by the very bed she lies on, dead?"

"Slander!" returned the other. "What's slander —lies? I've not spoken a lie, as I stand here, by the truth of God:

she was mine before she was yours, Captain Treherne; you only got her second hand."

At it again, locked, as you may have seen the statues of some wrestling gladiators of the olden time, who were bound together, to struggle until one was killed. But Sir Henry Griffyths and Mr. Treherne, began to be fearful for the consequences, and as the combatants stopped for one moment's breathing time, the former gave orders to the servants to seize the man, who went by the name of Coles; which they did from behind, pinioning his arms, in the grip of half a dozen, as good as his own. When he found he was captured, he became furious.

"She was mine," he shouted, with wild eyes glaring and lips dropping with foam. "She was mine, long before you had her—down at Chelton-Marsh, where we was bred. I told her I'd shoot her, if she married another man. I followed her here for it, but she wouldn't heed me."

"Will no one gag this madman?" exclaimed George Treherne, his face pallid with rage, whilst the perspiration ran off it like beads, and his lips quivered with his passion. "Will no one stop the mouth of this liar? Sir Henry, let me go! till I tear his tongue from out it."

But Sir Henry would not let him go, at that moment. He felt that George Treherne was almost as mad as his antagonist.

"Oh! you want to stop my mouth do you?" said the captured man, with malicious glee. "You don't want to hear about the 14th of July, do you, and how my lass and I, spent a night at sea together, hi an open boat? She loved me then, did my Nell. It wasn't a cold night, by no manner of means; but she didn't mind sitting close anigh me, didn't Nell, at that time, nor feeling my arms round her, nor my cheek against her own. Do you want to hear about that long summer's night, and what we said, and what we did? Shall I tell you, Captain Treherne?"

Luckily for John Read, more luckily still for George Treherne, Sir Henry's whispered orders had been obeyed by

this time, and a muffler procured with which to gag the unfortunate man; for they would not have found it an easy task to hold the insulted husband back much longer, and another encounter would have probably left the stain of blood on his soul for ever. As it was, when he saw his adversary at last well secured—his arms pinioned behind him, his legs fettered in like manner, and his stalwart form dragged off by the servants, to be safely locked up in a downstairs room, until the police should arrive to take him in charge—he grew calmer, and sitting down by the side of his uncle, laid his head on the bed, where the corpse of his unfortunate wife rested.

But the mischief was done. The murderer had said enough to convince all who heard him, that he had been one of the young mistress's former companions, and that there had been some good cause for jealousy between them. Sir Henry tried to do away the impression he had raised, by saying to some of the principal servants—

"Of course, you will not think of believing any statement, that poor creature has professed to make. He is evidently out of his mind, and if he had not shot your poor mistress, would have shot himself, or some of you. No one but a madman would have thought of returning to the scene of his crime, where he knew he must be discovered, and arrested. I suppose he climbed in at the open window. Take care uo one unlocks the door of the room where we have put him, until the police arrive."

Speaking thus carelessly, he kindly tried to cover the disgrace, which he felt the madman's words would cause henceforward to attach to the character of their dead mistress. But though the attempt was good, it utterly failed. From that day, the errors of Helene Treherne's former life were almost as well known to her domestics, as they had been to herself.

Left alone, for the servants had all followed Sir Henry Griffyths and the murderer, Mr. Treherne approached that part of the bed where his nephew had laid his head, and gently took his hand.

The young man returned the pressure, but he did not look up.

"George, my dear boy," said his uncle, "look at me. I want to speak to you."

He raised his head then, wearily, and his sad eyes met Mr. Treherne's. The latter pulled him up gently from his sitting posture, and tried to lead him to the side of the corpse; but he hung back and averted his face.

"George," said the old man, with impressive fervour, "I know how you must feel this, by my own feelings on the subject. It is worse than all the rest put together; but say you forgive her!"

But George did not speak, nor look round. His lip was nearly bitten through, as he stood with proud averted eyes, and his breast heaved, as he dwelt upon the newly-acquired knowledge of his injuries.

"Think of her mother, George. Think how she was left alone, brought up amongst the poor, without education or principle, and then think of her lying here, and say you forgive her!"

"Even the poor are sometimes virtuous," was the young widower's reply. "Uncle, the injury is greater than I deserved; it is the bitterest thing that has happened to me yet."

"She was very young, George, and the temptation to marry you was strong. Perhaps she also regretted it bitterly. Perhaps she suffered under the knowledge, as you do. She has paid the penalty for her folly, poor unhappy girl, with her very life. Cannot you forgive her, now that she is dead?"

Still there was no reply.

"Oh, George!" sobbed the poor old man, the tears which had been strangers to his eyes for so long coming down like rain, "she has gone to her God, with all her sins upon her head. Shall her husband's inability to forgive, add one more witness for her condemnation?" her death, from the effects of a gun-shot wound, inflicted on her by one John Head, *alias* Thomas Coles, whilst in an unsound state of mind." For there was no lack of professional evidence, to back up the unprofessional, in the assertion that John Read was completely, and hopelessly insane. A great sense of disappointment, and jealousy, aided and aggravated, by the drinking to which it had driven him, had destroyed the brain of one, who commenced life with every promise of being a great ornament, both in mind and body, in the class to which he belonged. So that not many days elapsed between the time when poor John Read—once so honest, so faithful, and so loving—was conveyed to a lunatic asylum, with no hopes of being loosed therefrom for life, and when the body of the woman, whose inconstancy had destroyed him, was laid to rest in the family vault at Ariscedwyn, and her widowed husband stood bareheaded beside her grave, and heard those blessed words of hope for all read over her, which had so touched his heart on another, and less engrossing occasion to him than the present.

"No," said George Treherne, softened by his uncle's grief, and the solemn truth brought before him. "Uncle, I had forgotten that!" and he stooped and kissed the corpse as he spoke. "God forgive you, Helene, as I do."

And then he sat down, and cried, and the reaction after his great excitement did him good. Having done what was necessary with regard to securing the murderer, Sir Henry Griffyths returned to the Blueroom, to try and persuade his friends to retire once more to rest.

Mr. Treherne was sitting by the bedside, but George was in the same position, in which he had left him. As Sir Henry Griffyths entered, he lifted his face, which still bore the trace of his unusual emotion, and said to him angrily—

"I'll never forgive you, Griffyths, for not letting me settle with that fellow; it's the worst turn you could have done me."

"Nonsense, my dear Treherne," was the answer. "What, let you be hauled up for manslaughter against a wretched lunatic, who didn't know what he was saying? You'll tell a different tale tomorrow."

"My mind won't alter against him tomorrow, or any day," muttered George Treherne, with set teeth; "he shall hang for this, by God!"

"Sir Henry," here interposed Mr. Treherne, "speak to him; do explain it to him. You heard that man's words; and though he is mad now, he was not so always. I understood them—we all did. Oh! my dear friend, this mustn't come to a trial; it would break my heart. I refuse to prosecute. Hanging the murderer, won't bring this murdered girl to life; and it will cast obloquy on our name. Grinyths, for his own sake, and mine, he mustn't prosecute; put it to him, in the proper light; there must be no trial."

"I don't think there would have been, in any case, my dear Treherne," answered the magistrate, kindly; "for the man is evidently mad, and we don't try madmen. We must get him put into an asylum, and then there will be an end of it."

"You should have let me deal with him," angrily interposed George Treherne; "his life was my forfeit. I suppose, if you both say so, that there will be no trial; but I should have been his executioner. By heavens! when I think of it, I feel as if I must go down stairs, and finish him as he lies."

But George Treherne did no such thing; his words were words of passion, not such, as in calmer moments, his humanity and justice would have dictated to him. But the morning brought him better thoughts—truer to himself—and he acknowledged the sense of not making a bad matter worse, for the sake of an unsatisfactory revenge. As Sir Henry Griffyths had said, and Mr. Treherne had wished, so it was; there was no trial. A second Coroner's Inquest assembled, before the body was laid in the ground, which proved a longer business than you would care to hear, or I to tell of, here; for witnesses were had from distant Chelton-Marsh, to swear to the identity of the man who professed to have been bred there; and Farmer and Mrs. Willis were amongst the number, and wept so much, and talked so much, about their foster-child in the servants' hall, and their suspicions for the reason of the murder, that the Trehernes were very thankful to get them transported back again to Chelton-Marsh. And then, after the several witnesses had deposed to their former statements, aided by the extra evidence of those who had captured the murderer, and heard him acknowledge his crime, the verdict given was: "That the deceased, Helene Treherne, came by

Mr. Treherne had been in his bed for several days previously, but he insisted upon getting up and accompanying the remains of his granddaughter to the grave; no entreaties on the part of his nephew, or Sir Henry Griffyths, had the least avail, so they stood together there, and together drank in hope for the dead, from the sacred words which the living read for their comfort. And whilst they stood at the open vault, the weather, which had been cloudy all the morning, suddenly changed, and one of those violent storms descended, which we often encounter in the hottest weather—rain and hail—which rattled down upon the frosted silver ornaments of the gorgeous coffin, and drenched the mourners to the skin. The widower's crape trappings clung in mournful folds about him, before the service was ended, and his handsome head was wetted through with the merciless rain. He was young, and strong, and did not feel it; but Mr. Treherne, who had only left his bed to attend the funeral, was thoroughly chilled throughout his weakened frame by the circumstance, notwithstanding all the care his nephew took to prevent it. Yet, in listening to those words, and trying to connect them with their thoughts of the departed, they had little time to think of anything else.

CHAPTER IX. ELFRIDA BETRAYS HERSELF.

How strange a thing it is in this world, that those we love best, can, when separated from us by only a few miles, suffer, sicken, even die, without any sympathetic feeling on our part, warning us, that part of ourselves has faded out of the world! Yet, so it is. Cases there have been, but so rare as to be almost unable to obtain belief, where kindred souls have received some token of their coming loss; but it is not the general rule. The creature we cherish most, whose

heart is one with ours, in whose life our own is bound, from whom we have never had a differing opinion, nor heard a differing word, may die away from our embrace, and in dying, call on us, with all the gathered strength of an expiring love, to come to them, only to come to give them one. last look, one breath, one sigh, that Love may go with them part of their dark way. And yet they call in vain. They pass out of this troublesome world, without the comfort of our presence, and we do not even know it. We sit at home, perhaps, pursuing our daily business or pleasures, and thinking of our beloved one as doing the same; never dreaming, never doubting, until the shock comes, the flood is on us, unawares, and every barrier of hope, and joy, and peace which this earth held for us, is broken down at once. But not for ever. Oh! thank God! not for ever! They may be a long time building up again, they may never be entirely rebuilt, but the flood, the overwhelming rush of waters, retires sooner, or later, and the way is passable. Else, how could we suffer as we do, and live?

On that fatal day in June, when that awful tragedy was taking place at Ariscedwyn, and the heart of George Treherne was too much occupied with the horror of the loss which had come upon him even to give a thought to his past troubles, Elfrida had spent, for her, an unusually happy and contented day. For she had been considerably happier since she had had that interview with him, at the garden-gate. Before that time, a fear that he misconstrued her motives, and doubted her affection, and by such doubt and misconstruction, might become reckless of doing right, had possessed her heart, and driven out her peace, as it had clone her happiness. But his last words had reassured her. As she had truly said to him then, her life would, thenceforth, be comparatively easy. To lose him for this world, she had made up her mind, as soon as she came to the full knowledge of what the loss would be to her; but to lose him for the world to come, she felt would have been beyond her strength to bear. But to know that he had learnt to read

her actions in their proper light—to acknowledge that she was right, to resolve to bear his share of the world's brunt manfully—Elfrida, when she thought of this, could not feel sufficiently thankful to heaven for the relief. But you do not suppose it was always peace? Harness is apt to gall when first put on, particularly if it be not well-fitted to the shoulder which bears it; and like all people, and especially the young, who have set themselves a difficult task to overcome, her views of its greatness, varied according to the state of her mind. Some days, it appeared at its very best. Duty was not so difficult, after all. Everything must be for the best that heaven ordains. Life was short at its longest, and prayer was such, a comfort, and a help. At such times, Elfrida would notice herself in the glass, and observe, with secret pleasure, how thin she was growing, and how her looks were ageing under her continual thought. Then, for the moment, life would appear nothing in prospect; a little space, that would soon pass and be gone; and under the vision of an eternal future, Elfrida's eyes would glow with anticipation, and she would live for the rest of the day in a kind of beatific dream.

But there were other days, when the twelve hours spun themselves out to twenty-four, and threescore years and ten, seemed as if it were an infinity of time, that would never end, and there was an unhallowed longing, to be with the one who occupied her thoughts, a wild wish to run away—to lose her identity—to live in any situation, amongst any class, so that she might only be near him, sometimes to see his shadow fall upon the grass, or to hear his voice, even though it only spoke to others. This was nature, and the other was grace, and the two held fearful conflicts in Elfrida's breast, as they will in all of us, until we die. But that day in June had been one of her contented days. It had been a warm sultry afternoon in Milborough, as it was at Aris VOL. III. N cedwyn, and Elfrida had been strolling about the shady cemetery, now a perfect garden of flowers, planted by loving hands upon the various graves, and had been looking at the little mound, underneath which her dead infant lay. Her husband was resolute, in not allowing her to go to the expense of putting up a stone, to the memory of the little one, who had been privately baptized by bis own name, nor even a railing to enclose the ground. He thought the idea as extravagant a one, as had been the putting on of crape and bombazine, to commemorate its loss, although the materials of Elfrida's dress had been nothing like those mentioned (but to men, all mourning must be crape and bombazine). Had he known of Elfrida's visits to the cemetery, although he could not have forbidden, he would probably have greatly ridiculed them; and yet she often went, and liked to go there. Not because she particularly lamented the death of her infant: the disappointment had been great at the time, but she would not have brought the blighted child to life again, if she could —life, as she had experienced it, seemed so little worth. But she had come to associate it with the blighted love, which had been buried with her baby; and when her tears welled forth, as she gazed at the little grass-grown grave which covered its remains, they rose for herself, and for George Treherne. On this afternoon, she had been thinking much of him, as she sat alone in the quiet cemetery: wondering how he got on in his new life; if he found it as hard as she did hers; and reflecting, with an inward satisfaction, that she was already beginning to be glad that he was married, glad that he had a motive for which to struggle with his feelings; that he would, some day, perhaps, possess nearer ties than herself, perhaps, even, deeper affections—occupied with such thoughts, she hardly observed how the time went, the afternoons had grown so long, until, on looking at her watch, she was surprised to see that it was past six o'clock, their usual dinner-hour; and she commenced to hasten back to the house. For, combined with Elfrida's want of affection towards her husband, there had been springing up lately, if possible, a worse feeling—that of fear. She was excitable and nervous by na-

ture, and he had made her thoroughly afraid of him; she knew that he had been spending the afternoon at Crossley with his mother, for he had taken the ponychaise for that purpose, directly after luncheon. Elfrida had offered to go with him; for with every fresh resolution on her part to press forward in the path of duty, and to endure, there came an honest desire, to make herself more agreeable to the connections, with whom she had allied herself by marriage; but "William had roughly refused her offer, and had gone alone. He might be back by the dinner-hour himself, or he might not; but if he were, and she was late, he would be very angry with her. This idea was uppermost in her mind, as she hurried home that evening—walking faster than was good for her weak state of health. But she need not have feared his displeasure, for when she arrived at the Lawn, and made inquiries concerning him, she found that he was not in the house.

"Not yet in, James?" she said to the servant, as she consulted her watch again. "Why, it is a quarter to seven, and dinner was ordered at six. Hasn't your master been home at all, this afternoon?"

"Mr. Treherne came in at his usual time, ma'am; but a note came for him from Sorel Cottage, and he went out again immediately, and has not been home since."

"From Sorel Cottage?" repeated Elfrida; "how very strange! I wonder what they can want with him there! Well! tell the cook to keep the dinner back, till your master arrives, and send Dawson up to me." And she passed to her dressing-room as she spoke. She was rather glad of the delay; no idea of being alarmed at the cause of it, entered her head. He was sitting talking with Agnes, or he had met some friends, perhaps, and had forgotten the time.

William Treherne, though so particular about his wife being punctual, was not always so himself. He would be back directly. In the meanwhile, she should have time to dress, for her husband always liked to see her dressed in the evenings. HI or well, he grumbled,

if Elfrida did not appear in a dinnerdress, to grace his dinner-table; so she let down her fair hair, and brushed it in loose curls over her shoulders, which had grown painfully thin lately; and then her maid entered, and her dress was changed, and she was ready. As she stood before her toilettable, thoughtfully turning over the bracelets in her jewel-box, she said to her—

"Did you hear why, they wanted Mr. Treherne at Sorel Cottage, Dawson?"

"Well, ma'am, Jane, she brought up the note, and she did say as she understood, it was some news from Ariscedwyn as had come this afternoon."

"News from Ariscedwyn?" exclaimed Elfrida. "What kind of news?"

"Well, ma'am," answered Dawson, with her mouth very much pursed up, as if she knew more than she told, "Jane *did* say, as she thought it was bad news; for Miss Agnes, and the old lady had been taking on dreadful, ever since the telegram came."

"A telegram?" exclaimed Elfrida, turning pale"Dawson, what was it? Tell me at once!"

But Dawson would not divulge; she thought she knew more than she told; but she was afraid of communicating the story, as it had got about amongst the servants, to her young mistress; so she denied all further knowledge of the contents of the telegram.

"I don't know nothing for certain, ma'am. Miss Agnes didn't tell Jane nothing, except that a message had come from Ariscedwyn with bad news, and she must fetch Mr. Treherne immediately. I didn't ask further."

"You can go, Dawson," said Elfrida, presently. "I want nothing more."

Alone, her fears knew no bounds. Bad news from Ariscedwyn! Could it be of *Mm f* Elfrida's thoughts flew to all kinds of horrors, until she could bear suspense and solitude, no longer, and descended to the lighted dining-room, to wait for her husband's return. But he was long in coming; eight o'clock chimed from the clock on the mantelpiece, and there were no signs of him. Then Elfrida rang the bell, and it was answered by the same servant who had let her into the house.

"James, did you hear nothing more than Dawson did, about this telegram from Ariscedwyn? I cannot imagine what keeps your master,away so long?"

The footman had been standing with the door in his hand; but at his mistress's question, he closed it carefully, and advanced a few steps into the room, with the air of one about to communicate an important secret.

"As far as I could understand, ma'am, from the woman who delivered the note, it was in consequence of a telegram, received by Mrs. Henry Treherne from Ariscedwyn this afternoon."

"Yes, yes, I know that," said Elfrida, hastily;. "but what was in the telegram? Did you hear that, James?"

"I understood that it was bad news, ma'am; that"—and here the footman's voice sunk almost to a whisper—" that some one had been shot, ma'am."

"Shot?" cried Elfrida, starting from her seat. « What, killed, James? Who? Old Mr. Treherne?'»

"Oh! no, ma'am, not old Mr. Treherne, I should think, but the young woman had not rightly understood who it was. The ladies were in great distress about it, and both the servants heard that there had been a murder committed, on somebody at Ariscedwyn, but they were not sure who it was. The ladies had not informed them, but they knew it was not old Mr. Treherne, because Miss Agnes mentioned him. Should I bring up the dinner, ma'am?"

"Oh, no!" said Elfrida, faintly; "wait till your master comes, James. That is all."

The man lingered about the room a minute, just to see how his mistress took the news, whilst he feigned to rearrange the salt-cellars, and to alter the position of the forks and spoons; and then he left the apartment again, closing the door softly behind him as he went.

As he did so, Elfrida buried her face in her hands. If she had felt fear before, what did she do now? Not old Mr. Treherne; who else could it be but— oh, no! that idea was too horrible; she would not, she must not, entertain it. And yet she did entertain it, in all its

worst shapes, until another hour had slipped away, and she heard the handle of the halldoor turn, and her husband's footsteps sounding in the hall. He threw his hat and gloves upon the halltable, and came straight into the dining-room. As he caught sight of his wife's figure, he started as if he had forgotten all about her, or the dinner-hour.

"Good heavens!" he exclaimed, "it must be late. Elfrida, have you been waiting long 7"

But she did not answer his question. As he entered the room, she had risen from her seat, and now advanced towards him, with a face of startling pallor, and trembling lips, which could scarcely form their words.

"William," she said, "what is it? Oh! tell me quickly."

He knew what she meant, and yet he answered, "What is what?"

".They say," she exclaimed, "that some one has been shot at Ariscedwyn. Who is it? For God's sake, let me know!"

Her anxious eyes were seeking his, as if life or death hung on his answer; her mouth was parted with suspense; her body was shaking with agitation. He saw it all, and he guessed the cause.

Now, William Treherne had been passing the afternoon with his mother and sisters, and he never returned from his visits to Crossley with very kindly feelings towards his wife. For his sisters disliked her, and let no opportunities slip of setting her actions in their worst light, before her husband. And on this particular afternoon, they had been discussing her steady refusal to go to Ariscedwyn on a visit, and making surmises as to her reasons for so doing.

"It is inexplicable to me," said the husband, in the course of the conversation. "She seemed so happy the last time she was there, always singing, or skating, or driving about somewhere; and now she is as obstinate about not going, as if it was the dullest place in the world."

"Captain Treherne was not married, the last time you were there, William," observed Dora, spitefully.

"What of that 7 asked her brother.

"What of that? oh you blind goose!" said his sister. "I really believe you think still, that George's intimacy with Elfrida was all friendship."

He really had believed it. Not on account of his faith in him, or her; but because, as I have said before, he was too careless of what happened to his wife, and too wrapt up in himself, to take the trouble to observe the danger she was in. But he did not like the remark that his sister had made now; he got very red, and looked very angry, and said, speaking also angrily—

"Who says it wasn't?"

Dora tossed her head, in disdain for his ignorance.

"I don't know who said it wasn't; but, I should think, every one could *see* that it wasn't."

"Every one means yourself, I suppose?"

"Myself, and mamma, and all the others; ask them yourself what they think, if you like. They all say the same as I do: that if ever a man was in love with a woman, George was with Elfrida."

It had cost Dora Treherne a good deal to arrive at this conclusion, but, having arrived at it, she revenged herself by making the most of it. It was not the first time by many, that she had said the same thing to her brother, and he told her so. But she referred the matter to her mother and sisters, and then the conversation became general, and everybody said what they thought; and William Treherne sat by and allowed the wife of his bosom to be discussed before him, until he got angry himself, and had sharp words with his relations, and left them in a huff. He was angry because their suspicions of Elfrida touched himself; not because he was indignant at slander, against a creature he loved. As he drove home, and brooded on all they had said, light seemed to break upon him, where he had before refused to open his eyes. Now that the subject was brought thus forcibly before him, he could see that it might have been so; and, in that case, that it accounted for his wife's unwillingness to visit the house, where his cousin spent his married life. These thoughts had not tended to increase the little feeling of affection he entertained towards Elfrida, and he had fully intended to accuse her of the fact, when they should next meet. But when he arrived at home, and found the note from Sorel Cottage, begging him to go there at once, the visit, and subsequent dreadful news of the murder of Helene Treherne, which had just arrived by a telegram from Ariscedwyn, had driven the thought of his wife out of his head. But when he returned to his own house, and she met him in that agitated manner, with hasty inquiries on her lips, and he found that her emotion was due to her uncertainty respecting the news which had been received, the remembrance of the conversation at Crossley flashed across his mind, and his own thoughts on the subject returned to him as well. As the nervous words, "For God's sake, let me know," left her lips, he turned upon her in a burst of passion.

"I know who you think it is. I know what makes you come shivering to me like that, and asking me to tell you at once. You think it's your *lover,* Mrs. Treherne, don't you? Ah! you thought I didn't know anything about that! You think I walk about with my eyes shut, *don't* you? It would have been ten thousand pities if he had been shot, wouldn't it? eh?"

As he ejaculated his string of questions, he walked restlessly about the room, only stopping every now and then, to give his wife a look of what was intended for cutting sarcasm; but it failed. He had told her, unwittingly, in his last sentence, what she had desired to know—it was not George Treherne who had been murdered. Elfrida breathed again, but even in her relief, she was so utterly taken aback by her husband's accusation, so astounded at his anger, that she could only stand feebly looking at him, and answering nothing.

"Well, what have you got to say for yourself?" he asked presently, in a voice of thunder, as he turned and confronted her. "Can you deny, that you have let that man make love to you?"

Then a thought rushed through her brain, a wild idea of throwing herself upon his generosity, and telling him all. Elfrida had a generous heart herself, and she judged others by it; and it was an impulsive heart also, and she acted on its impulse now; she spoke hurriedly, and with great excitement—

"William, if you ask me the question directly, I cannot deny it. You married me, knowing that I did not love you. Heaven knows, I could have loved you, if you had been kind to me; but that you never have been; and then you let me see him. Why did you bring us together? It was a fearful, a horrible risk. God knows I have suffered for it."

"Go on," said William Treherne, sneeringly; "finish your creditable relation, Mrs. Treherne."

"Why have you always been so hard upon me?" she said, deprecating his sarcasm, even in that moment. "I was very young; you might have remembered that, and been gentler and more patient with me; but you threw me upon strangers for love, and that was the end of it. Oh! William, do not look so terribly at me. I parted with him for ever, before he married; I have been thoughtless, but I have not been wicked. I am still your wife; oh, forgive me, William, and love me, and I will try to forget it all!"

Her beseeching looks, her lovely youthful face, drenched with her tears, her outstretched hands, had no effect upon him.

"I dare say you would forget, madam," he said; "sooner, probably, than I should; but I do not wish to interrupt your story. Pray let me have the sequel to your Platonic attachment for my cousin."

Her eyes flashed now upon him, through her tears, like living coals.

"There is no sequel," she said, "excepting that our hearts were broken. If I had wished to save mine from it, I should not be here now."

"A very honest confession, certainly," replied her husband, "and worthy of what preceded it. Perhaps, however, I am none the better for your being here. After what you have told me, however, I suppose you scarcely expect to remain?"

"Not remain?" she answered. Her eyes went wearily round the room, as if she scarcely understood him, or cared to understand.

"Do you hear me?" he said, his passion getting the better of him. "If you expect to remain in this house, after what you have told me to-night, you are greatly mistaken. You may think it play, to trifle with my name in this manner, and to let every one in Milborough know the story of your folly, but I don't. You shall leave this house to-night; one roof doesn't shelter you and me, again. I don't care where you go. To your father's, or to your sister's (who helped you doubtless to carry out your intrigue), or to the workhouse, or the streets—it matters nothing to me —but you shall go, and at once."

As he spoke she commenced to move slowly towards the door.

"It is just what I might have expected of you," she said. "It is all the same to me, whether I go or not. I ought to have known you have no pity. God have mercy on me!"

At her last exclamation, her husband's fury burst out afresh.

"Ay! this is what comes of your religion," he said; "to allow a man to make love to you under your husband's eyes. Fool that I was, not to have seen it before! I wish it *had* been *him* who had been shot; it would have been better work by half, —the dishonourable villain, the scoundrel!"

At this abuse of the absent man, she turned upon him like a fury. She was no longer Elfrida Treherne, she was some woman fiend, some incarnation of hate and vengeance and outraged love.

"He is not!" she exclaimed; "he is all that is good, and honest and true. If he was not honourable, he would have taken me from you." (Her affection made her forget how readily he once would have done so). "As it was, he left me, as I preferred to be left, to virtue and misery together."

"Very obliging of him, I am sure," returned her husband, "and considerate of you; but, as it happens, I am afraid it was lost trouble on both your parts, as I don't seem to care about retaining the blessing. You can pack your boxes as soon as you please, you can go where you like, but one roof doesn't shelter us two, to-night, or henceforward, for ever." He spoke with the greatest anger, and passing her, where she stood, left the room, and the house, at the same time. At first, she felt quite bewildered; then, as she remembered that she had betrayed herself for nothing, for worse than nothing, she was ready to curse her own folly for having spoken as she had done. She had thought to throw herself on his mercy, who had none—to break the ice between them, to effect a reconciliation, which should be the commencement of a new and more loving life. But she had mistaken the man she had to deal with. William Treherne had not the requisite generosity to understand such a confession on a woman's part, to

Vol. m. o answer such an appeal. It only made him harder against her. He laid the avowal to her being hardened on the matter, not softened, as was really the case.

But it was all over now. He had said that she should go, and at once, and Elfrida had too much pride not to take him at his word. She walked upstairs as if she was in a dream, and rang her dressing-room bell.

"Dawson," she said, as the maid appeared, "pack my boxes at once. I am going away." The woman stared in mute astonishment, but her mistress repeated the order. "Pack them at once—I don't feel well, and I don't want to be worried I am going to see a friend for a short time."

She was conscious that some sort of explanation was necessary to be given to her servants, but further than this she said nothing. The reason for the sudden resolve, for the strange hour of removal, she left them to find out for themselves.

"Am I to go with you, ma'am?" demanded the lady's-maid as she commenced to pack.

"No. I shall go alone. I am going on business that cannot be put off. Only pack one box; I cannot take a lot of things."

'-' Any evening dresses, ma'am *T*

"Yes. No. I don't care—put in what you like."

"Your jewellery, ma'am?"

"No, none of it." Elfrida had the bracelet with the diamond clasp, George Treherne's wedding gift, upon her arm at the time, and clasped it closer to her as she spoke. When the packing was concluded, and her dress changed for her walking things, she ordered them to get a fly, and when it arrived, walked down to it, and saw her one box deposited on the roof, as if she was only going for a little while, and would soon be back again. The servants were dumb with amazement; but as a false rumour of the fatal news from Ariscedwyn had got afloat amongst them, it was generally thought that Captain Treherne was the subject of the murder, and that their mistress was probably going to Ariscedwyn, to be with the young widow, and comfort her. It was a wild idea, but it was the only solution of the question they could arrive at. When Elfrida was asked where the fly was to be driven to, she said, the railway station, although she had no notion of the date of arrival or departure of the trains; but before they had got halfway there, she put her head out of the window, and stopped the driver.

"Do you know if there are any trains to London as late as this?" *She* asked, as he got off the box to inquire her wishes.

"Only one, miss " (every woman who wears a hat is "Miss" to a cabman and a shop-boy), "the mail train, and that don't reach Waterloo till past two—latish for you to be about."

She was very unused to travelling alone, and she felt it would be so, so she ordered him to drive to the principal hotel in Milborough instead—"The Eoyal Arms." The publicity of the act did not in the least trouble her. She must pass the night somewhere; that would do as well as anywhere else. Every one would know it soon, that she had separated from her husband, perhaps believe worse of her, so what could it signify? She seemed to have become quite dead to any sense of shame, or timidity. She had only one great idea in her head, that she was turned out of her husband's

house—when she had mastered that, it would be time to think of other things. On arriving at the hotel, she asked for a bedroom, walked mechanically to it, and sat mechanically in it until the morning broke, and Milborough High Street was alive again. Then she drove to the station and started for London, and from London she went to Edinburgh, and from Edinburgh to her father's address, in a village not many miles from that town. And she did this, fasting all the time. So that it is not surprising that, when she rushed into Grace's arms, frightening both her father and her sister by her unexpected appearance, she alarmed them still more by the incoherence of her words and attempted explanation. For Elfrida, from the combined effects of fasting, fatigue and mental excitement, had brought on a return of her old enemy, fever, and for many days after her arrival at Brackenburn, she lay blissfully unconscious of herself, the world around her, or her trouble.

CHAPTER X. CHANGE UPON CHANGE.

The morning after the funeral of his granddaughter had taken place, Mr. Treherne was again unable to leave his bed, and before the day was over, it was evident that he was really ill. His little remaining strength seemed to have deserted him; he complained of great pain in the chest and head, and his breathing was short and hurried.

George Treherne took alarm, and sent at once for the family doctor, who resided no nearer than Stokeley. As soon as he saw his patient, he pronounced the attack to be one of inflammation of the lungs, brought on by the exposure and chill of the day before acting upon a weakened constitution. For Mr. Treherne was an aged man now, past seventy years, and quite incapable of withstanding any shock to his bodily health. At first the doctor, Mr. Harris, spoke hopefully of the case, and the severer symptoms, indeed, soon disappeared under the treatment which he pursued, but the remedies were necessarily powerful, and the weakness which followed them was extreme.

On the fourth day, Mr. Harris begged

to speak to George Treherne alone.

"I have a painful duty to perform, Captain Treherne," he said, as the latter followed him into the dining-room, "and especially, coming as it does at so sad a time," he added, glancing at the deep mourning habiliments of the young widower;" but I suppose you are aware that this attack has left your uncle in a very weak state?"

George guessed the truth at once, and said so—that his uncle was going to leave him. He did not feel in the least surprised to hear it. It seemed now as if he had known it all along. The fact is, the life of excitement which he had led for the last six months, combined as it had been with mental trouble, had so wearied him, that he was scarcely capable of being startled or shocked any more. Besides, his uncle had been failing for some time past.

"You mean to tell me that my uncle is dying, Mr. Harris?"

"Mr. Treherne is in a very dangerous state, sir. He *may* rally; we are all deceived at times; but I think it unlikely. I have attended him for years, as you know, and his constitution has been gradually breaking up for the last twelve months. Late events have doubtless aided in further debilitating him. I am afraid I can hold out but little hope of his recovery."

"Have you told him so, Mr. Harris *T*

"No, Captain Treherne; your uncle did not mention the subject to me, and I did not feel there was any immediate necessity for breaking the news to him. Perhaps you will do so yourself."

"If he asks me the question, I will. I don't suppose *he* will care much, poor old man, either way. Well, it never rains, but it pours."

The expression was commonplace, but the deep sigh which accompanied it, made it sound anything but so. The doctor attempted some sentences, intended to be consolatory, but George Treherne rose to leave the room.

"Don't think me rude, Harris, if I go; I should like to be alone for a little while. I am not in the least surprised at what you have told me, but I didn't expect it just yet; and I feel it more, per-haps, than you would think."

He did feel it very much. He knew his uncle was an old man, and a weak man; but he had looked forward to his living many years at Ariscedwyn yet, living to welcome him back there, many a time to come. For, since his wife's death, George Treherne had had a mighty project growing up in his brain; a project which he had mooted only the night before, whilst sitting by his uncle's bedside. Mr. Treherne had lain for some time, watching his nephew, by the light of the night-lamp, neither reading nor writing, though materials for both lay before him, but sitting with his head on his hand, gazing fixedly at one particular spot on the carpet beneath his feet. He thought his mind was dwelling perhaps on the painful event which had just happened, and spoke to him, in order, if possible, to divert it.

"What are you thinking of, George?" But George never heard, and still continued gazing at the spot on the carpet. His uncle repeated the question, using his name first to attract him, and then the young man started, and looking puzzled, said— "What? eh? did you speak to me, uncle *T* "I have spoken to you twice," said Mr. Treherne; "but you were too occupied to hear me. What were you thinking of?"

"What was I thinking of?" echoed George, as he rose from his seat, and drew nearer to the bedside. "Uncle, I can't live this kind of life any longer; there is nothing to keep me here now, you must let me go."

"Where, George *T* demanded Mr. Treherne.

"Where? anywhere; so there is an object in my going, which requires both pluck and perseverance to cany it out. Here, I am, nearly thirty years old, and I have done nothing in my life but what I am ashamed of. I see other men around me, with objects in their lives—if it is only working for their bread—but mine has been objectless. What good have I been to any one? None."

"Don't say that, George," answered his uncle; "you have been the greatest comfort to me, all your life; and, until now, you had duties to keep you at home."

"Duties, yes; how did I perform them? If I had thought less of myself, and more of my wife—if I had tried to gain her confidence, I might have prevented that bloody murder. I feel as if half her death lay at my door."

Mr. Treherne was very much shocked at his nephew's self-accusation; he knew it was unfounded, and he tried to convince him of it, but in vain.'

"It's no good talking to me," was all the answer he got; "I feel I have wasted thirty years, but I will let the future redeem them, if I can. I may not have thirty more to spend as I like."

"What do you want to do, George?" asked his uncle.

"I want to go away, uncle, from England altogether, for a time. If I hadn't sold out, I might have got sent on foreign service; but I mustn't think of that, I suppose. What do I want to do? anything to be useful; head an exploring party for Government, or go and look after Sir John Franklin: it little matters to me: my head and my hands are at the world's service, but I must have *work.*"

"These late troubles have upset you, George, as they have me," said the old man, presently; "but it would give me a great deal of pain, if you were to leave England just now. I wish you would wait, George, a little, and not be in a hurry about it."

"I will wait, uncle, till you are well again, and then you must let me have my way, if you don't wish to see me go mad. Do you think I could sit down quietly *here,* in the very midst of the recollections of the past, and live upon you? Why, every leaf in that park, every stone on that road, would silently reproach me, each time I passed by them. No, uncle, I can't stop here."

"Poor boy, poor boy," said Mr. Treherne, taking the young man's hand. "Yes, George, I see it is best you should go away for a while—but not just yet — wait a little, for my sake."

And George had not only consented to wait outwardly, but had determined to do so also in his heart; although he panted to be up and doing. The dreadful death of his young wife had made a great impression upon him. It is true he had not loved her; that he had not striven (until just at the last) to gain her love; that he had often felt bitter and hard against her, and shown his feelings openly. That did not improve his reflections; it only made them more galling—more difficult to bear. He felt he could not live amongst the scenes of his married life, just yet. He felt he could not be idle, and enjoy himself, just yet. There was *that* in his past life which required purging; and, until it was purged by the commission of actions, greater and worthier than any it had given birth to yet, George Treherne felt that it was impossible for him to commence life anew. But he had not thought of the probable issue of his uncle's present illness, until the doctor brought it forcibly before him. Now, of course he must wait, even if his uncle rallied from this attack. He could not have left him to spend his last days alone, whatever he bore himself from the delay. But in two days more, all hope was past of Mr. Treherne's rallying, and he knew it himself. He had asked Mr. Harris for his candid opinion, and the doctor had given it. He was quite happy under the intelligence. As his nephew had said, it made little difference to him, either way. He was quite ready to go, as he would have been quite contented to remain, if it had been the will of Heaven.

"You see, George," he said to his nephew, the first time they conversed on the subject together, "that I was right in asking you to delay your departure for a little, wasn't I? You will soon be your own master now, and have no one to question your going or coming, except it is your mother. Always be kind to her, George; she has her faults, but a man can have but one mother, and she loves you."

"I know it, sir, and I have been greatly to blame in our various quarrels. It shall be so no more."

"Have her to live with you here, George, until you marry again; which you will do, please God, some day."

"*Never, uncle, never!*" The word was given twice over, with such emphasis, that the dying man opened his eyes in astonishment.

"You think so now, George, because all these things are so recent. I shouldn't have mentioned it, except that I shall so soon be past talking to you at all. It would sadden my last hours, though, to think you were in earnest."

At this assertion, George did not like to repeat his determination, although he did so in his heart. Presently his uncle went on—

"You will change your mind, by-and-by, George, and bring a nice wife home to Ariscedwyn, to be the mother of the future heir. George, you mustn't die without leaving an heir to the estate."

Still George was silent. He had no intention of bringing home a nice wife, or any kind of wife to Ariscedwyn, and he didn't know how the heir was to be managed without. But presently he answered—

"I will do my best for, Ariscedwyn, until I die, depend upon it. I shall never forget how dear it was to you."

"If you don't marry again," resumed the old man, "your sister's children will be next heirs. Ariscedwyn mustn't pass away from the Trehernes, George; promise me that."

It was an awkward promise to have to make, but George evaded it somehow, and his uncle was getting too weak to notice much what was said to him. Presently he resumed—

"George, I can't help thinking of Elfrida Treherne; she was always a pet of mine. I should like to have seen her again, but it little matters. I shall meet her hereafter. Is William kind to her, George?" "Not always, I am afraid, sir. " "She is very young, and she used to be so merry. Is she merry now, George?" And his nephew answered, in almost the same words—

"Not often, I am afraid, uncle;" and then added, "she is older, you know."

"Ah, true!" sighed the old man, "but she was such a wild kitten. I wonder why I think of her now that I am dying: but she was always a favourite of mine. George, take care of her after I am gone; don't let William ill-treat her." "How am I to prevent it, uncle?" "Be her friend, and his; and if there are quarrels between them, talk them into better minds. Have them down here often; they'll be nice companions for you."

"I can't do that, sir."

"You can't do that—why not?" demanded Mr. Treherne, fixing his eyes upon his nephew's face. George's eyes met his uncle's, and something in them told his secret. Past events, that had puzzled him at the time, became clear now to the dying man's mind, and he seemed to comprehend it all.

"Good God!" he exclaimed; "George, is it possible?" Eis nephew was going to deny it at first, or at least to waive the question, but he remembered that he spoke to the dying, and his false shame disappeared.

"It is possible, uncle, unfortunately," he replied. "I have never breathed a hint of it to another person; but the day I met Elfrida in this house, was the worst day of my life."

"How do you mean?" exclaimed the old man, seizing him by the wrist, as his nephew's words suggested a horrible idea to his mind. "George, you've never"

The other's eyes met his seriously for a moment, and then dropped.

"I know what you mean," he said in answer. "No, uncle, she's pure as snow; but it's not my doing that she is so."

"Thank God!" ejaculated Mr. Treherne, drawing a long breath. "George, you frightened me dreadfully."

"Cannot you account, sir, now, for all my past actions?' the young man went on hurriedly to say. "I met her, and loved her, too late. I was mad enough to tell her so, and make a rupture between us for ever; and, in my disappointment, I—I—"

"You married poor Helene. Yes, George, I see it all now—my poor boy—you must have suffered."

"I *have* suffered fearfully," said George Treherne, quietly; "but that is of little moment. You see now why I cannot be the friend to Elfrida that you would wish, and why I feel that my life is being wasted, until I can let her see, that I am striving by my future to redeem the past."

"I see, I see," murmured Mr. Treherne; "and that is why you are set against a second marriage, too, George—eh?"

"I could not marry again with my present feelings," said his nephew; "and I do not think they are likely to change. Time can only prove that, uncle: in the meanwhile, you will trust Ariscedwyn to me, with confidence, will you not?" VOL. III. P

"In perfect confidence," said the dying man. "Let it pass from the Trehernes, George, sooner than act against the dictates of your own heart; and God bless you, boy, whatever you do."

In a few more days, Mr. Treherne was gone, and the family vault was opened a second time within the fortnight, and George acted again the part of chief mourner, and returned to the large empty house, of which he was at last the owner, and felt, as he did so, that the possessions, the loss of which he had at one time so much lamented, had come to him too late.

The funeral of Mr. Treherne was a very quiet one. His cousin William was his next nearest relation to George, and the latter had written to request his attendance at the solemnity, but the letter did not reach him until after it was over. William Treherne had left Milborough by that time, and was in London or Paris, no one seemed quite certain where, and the postmaster had been left no authority to act upon. But George did not know of this until afterwards. The doctor, Mr. Harris, and Sir Henry Griffyths, were his only companions on the occasion, although there were plenty of empty carriages—respectful farces!— to follow the remains of the late owner of Ariscedwyn to the grave. The will was short and concise. All the personal property, excepting a few trifling remembrances to friends and old servants, was left without reserve to the heir, for his uDcle had made another will, as George knew, since the death of his granddaughter.

Well! it was all over. Everything seemed to be over to George Treherne just then—everything in life. His friends were not in the least astonished to hear him say that he intended to leave England for a while, and travel. They thought it the best thing he could possibly do. No one would have advised the young widower to stay on the spot where the misfortune of his life (as it was supposed to be) had actually occurred. So, not many days after his uncle's funeral, George Treherne called a meeting together of all his servants, and told them his intentions.

"I shall take care," he said in conclusion, "that Ariscedwyn is properly looked after in my absence; in the meanwhile, I look to every man here to do his individual duty to the estate. Although I am not present, remember that I am the owner of this place, and that I shall take a strict reckoning when I return, which may be at any time. Under ordinary circumstances I should have considered it my duty to remain amongst you; but, as things have happened, I do not yet feel able to look upon Ariscedwyn in the light of a home. In time, I shall trust to return to the old place, and be as good a master to you as my dear uncle was."

There were many tears shed at the young master's speech, and many oaths of allegiance to him taken on the spot; and George felt, as he shook the respectfully-offered hands of the older servants, that he was parting with real friends. He left them, followed by their blessings, and not without leaving behind him many a substantial proof of his acknowledgment of "their past fidelity. And in his generosity he did not forgot certain humble friends down at Chelton-Marsh. He could not bring himself to go there; there was no necessity for his doing so; but the effects of his liberal and substantial presents to the Willises, and through them, to all who had known and been kind to his late wife, were felt for many a hard season to come, in that poverty-stricken little hamlet.

Then he went to London, and let the first roughness of his grief wear itself off there, where, though he had a large circle of acquaintances, he could still be as much alone as he chose. And I think for a month or more, he scarcely stirred out of the splendid apartments, suitably correspondent to his recent accession of wealth, which had been secured for him at Mivart's Hotel.

In the meanwhile, the ladies of Sorel Cottage grumbled very much at the darkness in which they were kept, relative to his proceedings. Of course they had heard all about the murder of his wife, and he subsequent illness and death of Mr. Treherne. George had written them every outward detail of both circumstances in full, but no more. He could not enter into his own feelings on the subject of his wife's death to a third party. He could not even now think of the revelations of her.murderer, without a shudder. He pitied—he forgave her; but he could not love her memory; and, therefore, he was silent altogether. He said nothing of his own grief— nothing of himself. And his mother and sister attributed his silence to the excess of his sorrow. They were ignorant of the circumstances which had caused his marriage, remember—ignorant of his love for Elfrida. They felt with him greatly, the mother even more than Agnes; although with her distress she could not help mingling a feeling of triumph at her *r* son being master of Ariscedwyn after all. And she wanted to see this important personage now, to see how he comported himself under his new dignities— to ask him how he felt as a rich man.

But the rich man would not come near them. They wrote and asked him again and again, but he had always some excuse for not going to Milborough. He had engagements, business or otherwise, he was not well, he was coming next week; anything but coming at once. At last Mrs. Treherne got quite annoyed at his seeming indifference on the subject, and ceased asking him altogether—almost ceased writing. But Agnes still corresponded with him. In one of her letters she said—" *En passant,* have you met William anywhere in London? There are numberless letters lying for him here, that the postman keeps continually bringing to us, but none of his servants seem to know his address; and I have written to Elfrida for it, but have received no answer. I suppose you know she is with her father in Scotland."

Late the next evening, when Mrs. Treherne and Agnes were thinking of going to bed, he unexpectedly walked in. At first sight he seemed so altered that even his mother was startled to see him. It was not only that he had grown very pale and thin, but there was an appearance of age about him which George Treherne had never worn before. The care and the thought he had undergone, had drawn deep lines about his eyes and face, and the dbonnaire air which had always distinguished him, which used to be, as it were, behind even his most serious moods, was gone altogether—washed away by unshed tears. But the women noticed none of this to his face; they were not so devoid of tact: they only welcomed him heartily, although their welcome was, naturally, not unmixed with a little agitation. Mrs. Treherne was very eager in her inquiries about the estate, and her son's plans, to all of which he gave very curt answers, and as if his mind was much preoccupied.

Presently he said, sitting down between them, as he refused to eat the supper which they had had brought up for him—

"Mother, I couldn't come down here before for various reasons; and now I am come, I am afraid I bring, what you will call, bad news. I cannot stay, for I am going to leave England almost immediately."

"Leave England," said his mother. "Good heavens, George! why?".....,

But Agnes only drew her chair closer to his, and took his hand in hers, whilst she looked anxiously in his face.

"Look here, mother," he said in answer. "This news from India calls on every man who has a pair of arms, to help and revenge the wrongs of a nation. I have lived a wretchedly useless life hitherto; but there is work before me now. I have volunteered to go to Bengal with the Boyal Buffs, and they sail next week."

The intelligence fell on his mother and sister like a thunderclap. The Mutiny had just commenced in India at that time, and every mail brought home fresh accounts of barbarities practised on our unfortunate country-people—accounts which had curdled the blood of these two women, as they had the blood of all who possessed hearts to feel; and Mrs. Treherne and Agnes had heard of many acquaintances of their own, volunteering for the service of avenging the murder of England's defenceless ones, with pride in the thought that Englishmen so soon responded to a call for valour; but it had never entered their heads, that their only one, the head of their house and sum total of their glory, would enlist himself in so bloody and dangerous a cause. The voyage, the climate, the chances of war—all to be encountered together—poor Mrs. Treherne, when she thought of it, could only lay her head down on her son's knee and sob without restraint. He was touched at her evident grief, and raised her tenderly.

"My dear mother," he said, "my life has been too soft and easy hitherto; it has led me into sins which I shudder to look back upon. I have experienced a great loss" (his heart flew to Elfrida as he said the words, but his hearers only thought of his wife's death)," and England and idleness are alike distasteful to me for the present. It is only in work that I can ever hope to forget, and what more glorious work could you wish me to have, than that before me?"

"But Ariscedwyn," sobbed Mrs. Treherne; "surely, George, it is your duty to live on your estate, and look after it?"

"I could not live at Ariscedwyn just yet," he answered.

Then they remembered, and ceased to press him.

"What do you intend doing," presently asked Mrs. Treherne, "about the estate?"

"That is what I have come down chiefly to speak to you about," he answered. "Mother, do you love me?"

The sudden question was earnest, and touched her in like manner.

"Oh, George," she said, as she turned and folded him in her arms, "you know I do, my dearest son."

"I don't want to distress you unnecessarily," he went on to say, "but I must remind you, mother, as we sit here, that when we part, it may be for ever. I shall be as careful of myself as I possibly can, for your sake; but we go to war, and we are a handful opposed to thousands. I may never come back. Will you grant me a favour before I go?"

"Yes, dearest, anything," said Mrs. Treherne, as well as she could speak through her tears.

"Make up this quarrel between yourself and Lady Digby, and let Agnes and Charles be married in six months' time. Come, mother, it is but a little stifling of your pride, and the thing is done. I may never make you another request."

Mrs. Treherne was an obstinate woman, but she was also impulsive; and just now, as it happened, her son had taken her in an impulsive mood. She was thoroughly softened at the idea of losing him, perhaps altogether, for he was her idol as we know, and she dared not refuse him even this. Agnes was about to request that her affairs might not be made a subject of discussion between them at the last, but her brother stopped her.

"Agnes, I have set my heart on this. Mother, is it to be, or not?"

"Yes, George, I will do it". I will write to Lady Digby to-night."

"God bless you!" he said, turning suddenly to her, and laying his head on her bosom. "Mother, I feel as if I never knew how much I loved you till now, when I am so soon to lose you."

Agnes slipped out of the room, and George Treherne lay for many hours, as he had placed himself, on his mother's breast; his eyes, with their wonderful powers of fascination, gazing up into hers, whilst her tears fell fast on his handsome head. What confidences passed between them during those last sad hours I know not, but after George's departure from England, Mrs. Henry Treherne became very tender in her treatment of his cousin Elfrida, and made that poor child's heart often rejoice, under the influence of her kindness, and never-varying friendship. Before Mrs. Treherne parted with her son that night, she wrote the letter of apology to Lady Digby, in which she concluded by asking the sanction of herself and Sir Charles, to the engagement of her daughter and their son. Charles Digby was staying on leave with his parents at the time, but it was not long after the letter reached the Priory, that he showed himself at Sorel Cottage, and was received very graciously by Mrs. Treherne. Sir Charles and Lady Digby were thoroughly kind-hearted and goodnatured people. They would no more have dreamt of disregarding such an appeal on the part of Mrs. Treherne, than they would have thought of trampling upon a dead body; so that not long after George's departure to India, they also found their way to Milborough, and the poor mother, in her first sorrow at parting with her son, found her best comforter in the kind-hearted Lady Digby.

But in the meanwhile the Royal Buffs' hour for sailing, drew very near.

"Mother," said George, in arranging his affairs, "I wish you to live at Ariscedwyn whilst I am away.. K I thought Charles would be happier out of the army, I should advise him to sell; but I am sure he would not. Have them down there as much as ever you can, and spend my money as if it was your own."

"But, George"—remonstrated Mrs. Treherne.

"What need have I of thousands?" he returned. "I shall have more than I can spend as it is. I have engaged a first-rate bailiff to see after the estate; you need have no trouble about it, unless you choose. Keep up the name of Ariscedwyn for hospitality, mother; don't let me get a name for illiberality."

"I shall have no interest or pleasure in giving parties, dear George, when you are away," said his mother.

"Then let Agnes do it for you, mother, and do it well; and, above all, look to my tenantry, and the poor of the village. Let my money do some good whilst I have it. I leave it all to you, because I am sure I could not have a better almoner. Agnes, darling, I hope you will be very, very happy. It vexes me not to have been able to give my only sister away; but whoever does so, you must

fancy is your brother."

"Oh, George! I should much rather wait till you come back," said Agnes, weeping.

"Nonsense, child, that may never be. Besides, I feel as I should never be in place at a wedding again. You'll be an old married woman when I come back, dear, and have lots of nephews and nieces to introduce to me."

"I am so sorry Elfrida is not in Milborongh," said Agnes, "to wish you good-bye. I think she will be so vexed when she hears you are gone. Have you written to her, George?"

"No, I have not. I leave that to you, Agnes. Be a friend to her whenever you can. And now, God bless you, dear, and good-bye!"

These were some of his last words to them. In a few hours more, he was standing on board the " Bellepheron," bound for Calcutta, and only his friend Charles Digby left, to say farewell to.

"Look after my mother, Charles; she will miss me sadly. If I never come back, old fellow, Ariscedwyn will be yours, with Agnes; and may it be your son's son's, to a thousand generations!"

"Nonsense, Treherne, don't talk like that; you'll come back safe enough, old fellow; there's not much chance of *my* son's getting Ariscedwyn."

"Isn't there?" said his friend, thoughtfully. "Perhaps its wrong to say so, Charles, but I don't think it will make much difference to me, if I come back, or not."

Aud Charles Digby, hurrying back to Milborough a short time afterwards, thought to himself, that his wife's death seemed to have cut up Treherne frightfully, and that he had no idea he would have felt it so much. And George Treherne, the while, was standing on the deck of the "Bellepheron," as she slowly steamed out of the harbour, and left the shores of England behind her. What was he thinking of? Did he regret, now that it was too late, that he had left his native country, without one parting word, one farewell look, from the woman he loved?

No; he was going forth to danger, perhaps to death; his heart was un-

changed towards her, but so was his determination to do right. He never faltered in his purpose, he never wavered in his will.

"I cannot trust her with myself," were his thoughts, as the last piece of shore became a thin line in the distance, " but I can trust her with God;" and then, as it totally disappeared, he turned away, and sought his own cabin. "The bitterness of death is past," flashed through his mind as he did so. "Now for hard work, and plenty of it." CHAPTER XI.

AT THE HERMITAGE.

When Dr. Salisbury had taken his daughter Grace to visit their friends in Edinburgh, he had had no intention of settling out of England. But he was Scotch, and such of his relations as were left to him were all living in Scotland; and as he visited with Grace from one house to another, and entreaty followed entreaty that he would take some little place for himself, and settle down near them, he began seriously to entertain the idea. He had not been able to make up his mind before, as to where he should live. The world was all before him where to choose, and under such circumstances, choice is no easy matter. There are so many nice places in dear Old England and her sister countries, so many delightful nooks for old Indians to retire to, so many smiling valleysj and breezy hills, bold pieces of sea and placid rivers, that directly one has fixed upon one place of residence, another is immediately recommended, warranted to surpass the first in advantages. But Dr. Salisbury felt, as we all feel when we have made the trial, that it is not *where* you live that so much signifies, as *who* you live with. Without friends, the most charming paradise becomes a howling desert; and Dr. Salisbury had passed so much of his life in India, that he had few acquaintances left, and such as were left were in his native country. And so, as Grace was quite agreeable (for Dr. Salisbury would not have thought of taking any step in the matter without consulting his daughter), he decided to yield to the solicitations of his friends and look out for a residence amongst them that might suit him. And such a one was not long forthcoming, situated in a village called Brackenburn, not many miles from Edinburgh. For Dr. Salisbury stipulated it should be in the country: he had lived too long in a town, and was too used to the sight of stone walls, not to make him sigh for some quiet nest, far away from all such, and surrounded by English scenery. And the "Hermitage" seemed made for him. It was a pretty house, with a thatched roof and gables, which looked as though it was oldfashioned, but had in reality been built by some Vol. m. Q gentleman of property to gratify his own fancy. The inside, though not very large, was quite large enough to hold Dr. Salisbury's family with convenience, and leave more than one spare bedroom for his friends, besides possessing several large, and welllighted sitting-rooms. The garden in which the Hermitage stood, was extensive and well stocked, whilst the coachhouse and two-stalled stable was quite sufficient to hold the pony which drew their modest phaeton, and the steady cob on which the Doctor loved to make excursions almost daily into Edinburgh.

Altogether they could scarcely have done better. They were within an easy distance of one of the first towns in Great Britain, and of most of their friends. Grace was enchanted with everything in Scotland, and quite happy in her new home, and her father was contented in seeing her so. The accounts from Douglas Cameron were very cheering. He was working hard at his profession, was well in health, and anticipating a speedy return to his affianced wife. His friends, as his name denoted, were also Scotch, and Grace had already been introduced to them, through him, and had made a very favourable impression upon her future connections, and so for her, for the present, life was running smoothly enough.

The surprise of both Grace and her father, when Elfrida arrived so unexpectedly at the Hermitage, can be better imagined than described. The news of the murder of Helene Treherne had not yet reached them; and, if it had, they would still, of course, have been totally at a loss to trace any connection between that circumstance and the sudden appearance of Elfrida at their house; for the poor girl arrived too ill to be able to explain her reason for coming, with anything like coherence. A long night and day spent in rapid travelling, without breaking her fast, and with a great grief pressing on her brain, had been too much for Elfrida, in her weak state. Unintelligible accounts of unkindness, quarrels, and abuse, mixed up with expressions of pity and horror for some one shot or murdered, and vehement asseverations that separation was for life, were all that she was capable of telling them, and they conveyed little meaning to her hearers' minds, and had no effect, except that of frightening them. But one thing they knew and saw for themselves—Elfrida, their youngest, most cherished and best, had arrived, thrown upon their care, alone, ill, and evidently unhappy. When they found how much she needed rest and medical attention, she was put to bed at once; and then Dr. Salisbury turned to Grace, to give a solution of the mystery. But Grace was as mystified as himself.

"You had better write to William, papa, it is the only thing to be done. He will be able to tell us the reason of it all."

And therefore William Treherne was written to, and before an answer could be received from him the Salisburys had read the account of Mrs. George Treherne's death in the public papers; and Grace had listened to ravings from her sister's mouth, which told her plainly all she wished to know.

But these she kept to herself, and waited with her father anxiously for the reply to come from Elfrida's husband.

When it arrived, it was very unsatisfactory. Mr. William Treherne refused to satisfy Dr. Salisbury with the reason of his wife having quitted his protection, as she was the best person to inform him. He referred Dr. Salisbury, therefore, to Mrs. Treherne. "It was sufficient for him to say, that the separation had taken place under such circumstances, that it was impossible his wife should ever return to live with him again. He intended making her an allowance, (here a very small sum for such a purpose was named,) and she could do as she chose with it. Live with her father if he liked to keep her, or by herself —anywhere but with him."

To this letter Dr. Salisbury sent an indignant answer. The allowance offered, he refused to allow his daughter to accept, in terms of the supremest contempt, nor would he permit her to be beholden to her husband or his relations, for anything. Mrs. Treherne, he added, was not in a fit state to give any explanations of her reasons for leaving her husband, but as soon as she was—if it was proved that he had turned her out of his house without sufficient good reason for so doing—he might expect to be called upon to answer for it, in a much more public manner than the present; and he desired to know if Mr. Treherne was ready to come forward in such case, and give proofs that he had acted, in this instance, from justifiable motives.

But to this letter Dr. Salisbury never got a reply. William Treherne had shut up "the Lawn" for an indefinite period by the time it had reached its destination, and had gone upon the Continent with some bachelor friends. In the meanwhile, Elfrida was lying in Grace's bed, tossing about in a high fever,, rambling on, as the delirious will, sometimes of the subject which distressed her, sometimes of matters perfectly irrelevant to that, or any tiling connected with it, and then shuddering as under a great fear, and calling to Grace to come and hold her hand before her eyes, that she might not "see it." Several days and nights passed like this, and then her youth triumphed again, and the fever was gone, and Elfrida lay on her pillows as before—very weak and pale, but convalescent. The first day that she was sensible she said very little, and that little bore no allusion to herself; but on the second, she had been following Grace about the room with her eyes for a long time, until it seemed as if she could keep silence no longer. Then she said

"Grace, dear, come here."

Her sister was at her side in a moment, ready to listen or to speak, as was required of her.

"Grace, dear, it was not him, was it? you are sure it was not him T

Thinking she meant her husband, Grace said, inquiringly—

"William, dear?"

"William, no!" (the tone in which she pronounced his name, though weak, was one of withering scorn). "I was going to ask about George; but I remember now, he said it wasn't him who was shot."

She lay back her head, and closed her eyes, as if she was too languid, even to feel glad at the remembrance. She was in that state of extreme debilitation when we are unable either to weep or rejoice, when memory is gone, and almost sensation. But light flashed through Grace's mind at her sister's words, and she hastened to disabuse Elfrida's mind of the false impression, which she imagined might have caused her illness.

"Oh, no, dear Frida," she exclaimed; "it was not Captain Treherne, it was poor Helene; but we have heard no particulars. You didn't fancy it was any one you cared for, did you, Frida?"

"No," she answered, languidly; "I had forgotten; I seem to have been asleep for so long."

She did not express any new horror, or surprise, at the news of Helene Treherne's death; all her powers had been expended in her delirium.

"Grace, I am never going to live with my husband any more." This assertion startled Grace a few minutes afterwards, when she thought her sister was asleep again.

"Nonsense, Frida, dear, it will be all right byand-by," she answered; "try not to think abput it now."

But the denial roused Frida's energy, and she became excited.

"I shan't," she said determinately. "Grace, he knows all about George."

"Good heavens, Frida, who told him?" exclaimed Grace, in a dismayed tone, for she feared the friendship with George Treherne had gone further than she knew of, and this new avowal solved all the mystery of the quarrel between Elfrida and her husband.

"I did," said her sister, quietly; "he half guessed it, and I thought he would pity me if I told him the truth; but he had no pity, he turned me out of the house. Oh! Grace, isn't it cruel, isn't it hard? I had given George up. I had done all I could. God might have spared me this extra punishment."

Her tones were so bitter, that they shocked her sister.

"Elfrida," she said; "you mustn't question God's right to punish you. It may be a great trial, dear; but it is God's will."

"God's will—yes—but why should He delight in making me wretched? Oh! Grace, I loved him so, my heart was wrapt up in him. If I had not wished to do what was right, I should have gone away with him for ever, from all my misery; but I gave him up. I nearly broke his heart and my own too; and I was trying so hard to forget him, and to do my duty to William, and this is my reward. Turned out of my husband's house, as if I was everything that was bad; disgraced before my own servants—before all my friends. Oh! Grace, I shall never get over it. I hope I may never get up from this bed again. I hope I may lie here till I die!"

So she said in the sharpness of her pain, as the thought of her trials came back upon her reawakened memory. Grace was very much hurt at her sister's words, and showed her that she was so.

"Elfrida," she said, "I can hardly believe that it is my sister who is speaking in such a sinful manner; my Elfrida, who was taught with me, to regard everything that Heaven sends, as best, however painful."

"It is all very well talking," said Elfrida, gloomily; "you should try life as I have tried it, Grace. I haven't had a happy day, I do believe, since I was married: and now, when I have had such a hard struggle with myself, and have been praying and praying for months, that William and I might grow to like each other, and live a little more happily together, this is the end of it. God could have incliued my husband's heart to me if He had chosen. It is very hard, it is bitterly hard to bear. I feel as if I could

never try to do what's right again in this world, nor pray again, either."

There was silence between them for a few minutes, and then Grace's gentle voice said—

"Frida, when you prayed for yourself and your husband, what used you to pray for T 'For happiness between us, of course," answered Elfrida, rather testily: "that he might grow to love me, and that I might do my duty, and—forget!"

"Did you ever stipulate with God in what manner He should answer your prayer, dearest?"

"No, Grace; why?" And Elfrida's eyes opened with surprise as she spoke.

"And you were led on by circumstances to tell your husband of your unhappy attachment for his cousin, and to tell him, at the same time, that you regretted it, and wished to overcome it?"

"Yes! At least, I am sure I said something like that, only I cannot quite remember what passed between us."

"How do you know, Elfrida, that this very rupture may not be the means by which God is going to answer your prayer? How do you know that this separation may not be the *only* means by which your husband would have come to think of you, and care for you as he used to do? for I am sure he loved you at first, Elfrida."

"I don't believe he ever did," said Elfrida; and yet she looked pleased at Grace's assertion, and her sister saw it.

"Well, I am certain that he did," she repeated. "Perhaps there has been something wrong in your own conduct, Elfrida, which has alienated his love for a time. You have done him a great wrong. I don't wonder at his being angry—at his not being able at once to tell you he forgives you. He trusted you, Erida, and he trusted his cousin. It must be very hard to find he has been deceived."

"I didn't think *you* would have gone over to his side, Grace," remarked Elfrida, sadly.

"No more I have, dear," answered her sister. "I see all his faults better than I can see yours, because I do not love him so well; but here, I say he has had just cause for anger; some would say, just cause for a separation."

Elfrida's tears began to fall fast.

"You are all against me," were her words, " except one," she added, in a whisper.

"Oh, Frida!" exclaimed Grace; "don't say that, darling, when I would do anything to see you happy. But in this you must be patient, and leave God to work out His blessings in His own way. Don't leave off praying, Frida, don't leave off hoping, and it will all come right at last. It always does for those who pray and hope."

But the nights were the trying times for poor Grace. When her sister's delirium would return, and she banished all help from the sick room, that the burden of her rambling talk might not get repeated by the servants, and took the heavy task of night-nursing upon herself; and then was roused three or four times from her own sleep by Elfrida's scream of terror, and running to her bedside, would find the wretched girl, streaming with perspiration from every pore, and trembling from head to foot with fancied fright.

"Grace," she would exclaim, as well as her chattering teeth would allow her, "he is there; he won't let me stay with you any longer; he is going to turn me out again! Why doesn't he speak? Why does he stand so silently, and look me through and through? Oh, Grace! his arm is up, he will strike me! Oh, hold me close!"

And then she would sob and moan in her sister's arms until she had exhausted herself with weeping, and would lie back on her pillows in a sort of syncope. And as soon as she thought Elfrida was asleep again, Grace would creep on tiptoe back to her own bed, noiselessly as she could, in the hope of procuring some rest; but if by chance she closed her eyes, it was only to be roused again by hearing her name called, in the strange voice which sleep-walkers and delirious people use, and perhaps to answer some startling question.

"Grace, Grace! Why does George follow me here? Why doesn't he stay at Ariscedwyn with his wife? William will be angry again. They will quarrel. Tell

him to go back, Grace. I mustn't speak to him, indeed I mustn't. Oh!" Elfrida would shudderingly exclaim, as she came to herself, and knew what she was saying, " I wish I didn't dream of him, it is so wicked; but I can't help it, Grace. Don't let me go to sleep again."

And then poor Grace would bring out some book, generally the greatest Book of all, and force her wearied eyes to bear upon the page by the aid of the night-light, as she read in her soft voice such passages as she thought would comfort and soothe her sister's mind, until Elfrida's hand would relax its tightening hold upon hers, and her beautiful head would sink back upon the pillows again, overcome by drowsy weakness.

But when the day broke, and the terrors of mind she suffered by night were partly dispelled by its cheerful light, Elfrida was able to speak quite calmly and sensibly of her trouble. And as the days went on, her feelings lost much of the rancour and bitterness with which she had at first alluded to it.

When she was recovered from her illness, she made no scruple of telling her father her whole history, as I have told it to you, though it was often interrupted by tears of self-reproach and self-pity. As Dr. Salisbury listened to it from those girlish lips, and, remembering his doubts and scruples on and before the wedding-day, connected them with the wreck his daughter was now, he ground his teeth together and clenched Ins hands whenever the name of William Treherne sounded from her mouth, as he thought of the manner in which he had fulfilled the vow he had taken, to protect and cherish the young creature before him. But Elfrida was only anxious lest her father should believe, as her husband had done, that there was any sequel to her sad story, except that of her present wretchedness.

"Papa," she said timidly, when she had concluded, "*you* believe, don't you, that I have told you all? I have been very weak and wrong, I know, but I have not been so wicked as that. If it had been only my own happiness I had thought of, I do not know what it might not have ended in; but I could not, lov-

ing George as I did, have consented to anything which should have lowered him in his own eyes, or have brought down God's anger upon him, because," she added simply, " I really loved him, papa: it is my only excuse."

"Oh, Elfrida!" exclaimed Dr. Salisbury, taking the girl's slight figure in his arms, "why had you not a husband you could love? A heart like yours was never intended to be wasted."

"It is not wasted, papa," she answered eagerly; "I have you and Grace still left to me."

But to all her father's and sister's entreaties that she should write and attempt to justify her conduct in her husband's eyes, she always returned a decided negative. There was a great deal of pride in Elfrida's heart, and it made her very obstinate on this point. He had disbelieved her once, why should he not do so again? He had told her that one roof should never cover them henceforward, for ever; she would not risk the dread of a refusal. Besides, she did not wish to return to him; she would not if she could. And yet Grace knew that Elfrida, in saying so, did not speak the truth. Her melancholy by day they might attribute to any cause they chose; but her sister often heard her sobbing in her sleep, when the broken words upon her lips were not the name of George Treherne, nor of anything connected with him. She marked the feverish anxiety with which Elfrida awaited the arrival of the one daily post which came to Brackenburn, and the despondency which settled over her when day after day passed by without bringing her any letter—from whom?

With George Treherne she bad never corresponded, and soon the news of his departure from England reached them; but when the excitement of that was past, the feverish anxiety for letters still remained. And so the summer days slipped away, and three months had elapsed since Elfrida came to the "Hermitage." Three long months: surely time enough to deaden the first great aching pain which had accompanied her there. Three months, and though her fragile form, looking taller than heretofore from its extreme slightness, might be seen walking about the flower-garden of the "Hermitage," or reclining by Grace's side, as she drove her through the lanes of Brackenburn in her pony-chaise, still the lapse of time had brought little variation to the settled expression of sadness in her eyes, or colour to that cheek, the outline of which was so sharply defined by the attenuation of her face.

She liked to talk with Grace about her own prospects, and to have Douglas Cameron's letters read to her, and to have his character discussed, and his features described, for she only retained a faint recollection of him herself. Grace, at first, had forborne to speak of him, lest the contrast between her own expected marriage, and her sister's might strike the latter too painfully. But Elfrida was free from anything like jealousy. If she compared their fortunes at all, it was only to rejoice that her dear Grace's was so much more hopeful than her own. She seldom mentioned George Treherne's name now; only once, when Grace had suddenly stopped in the midst of some of her joyous anticipations, had Elfrida said—

"Go on, Grace, dear; never mind me. I can see now, that it is doubtless for the best for George Tre VOL. III. B herne and myself, that things have turned out as they are. If we had met sooner, as you and Douglas have done, when we were both free, we might have been so well satisfied with this world, that we should never have thought of another. I am quite contented, Grace, with respect to-him, indeed I am; and perhaps even the other may come right, as you say, in time. So tell me all you can about your pleasant prospects."

But "the other" seemed a long time coming right. All this while nothing had been heard of her husband. Of course, her sudden departure from Milborough had not been uncommented upon; but whatever conclusions her various friends there, arrived at as to the reason of her flight, were entirely owing to their own conjectures, for William Treherne never deigned to enlighten any one of them upon the subject of his do-

mestic affairs.

Agnes and Dora still continued to correspond with Elfrida, and it was from the former that she had heard all the particulars of Helene Treherne's death, and her husband's subsequent departure for India; but they neither of them ever alluded to any but the most ordinary motive for Elfrida's visit to Brackenburn. And of her husband's doings she was kept wholly ignorant, except such knowledge as she gleaned from chance sentences in his sister's letters; but she said she cared as little as she knew.

And, in the meanwhile, the world went wearily on at Brackenburn, Ariscedwyn, and Milborough, and Time's wheels seemed clogged with heavy shackles for all those who had been in any way connected with George and William Treherne.

CHAPTER XII.

A SLIP ON MONT BLANC.

But though Elfrida heard nothing, and said that she cared as little, about her husband at this time, it is necessary I should trace some of his movements, before I can again take up the thread of her own share in this story. When William Treherne returned to the Lawn, the night on which his wife left it, he was at first astonished to find that she was really gone. At the moment when he had told her that one roof should never cover them, thenceforward for ever, he had meant what he said; but he scarcely expected that Elfrida would take him so immediately at his word, and quit his protection without any further explanation or understanding, without any attempt at justifying her conduct in his eyes, or at bringing about a reconciliation between them. And to find she had done so, considerably piqued him, and made him feel small in his own eyes. She was very young, and very inexperienced, to be travelling about alone, and unprotected j but he could not' have followed her, if he had wished to do so; for, after his first betrayal of ignorance at her actual departure, he was shy of letting his servants know that he was equally ignorant of her destination, and so he could not question them as to what

direction the fly had been ordered to take their mistress. To their information that Mrs. Treherne had left the Lawn an hour previously, he returned a careless "All right," and never alluded to the subject again before them. And then came the letter from Dr. Salisbury asking for the explanation Elfrida was unable to give him, of the reason she had left her husband's house for his; and when William Treherne found that, instead of wandering about the streets, protectorless and exposed to danger, she was comfortably housed at the Hermitage, and had already able cudgels taken up in her behalf, his indignation against her returned, and he answered Dr. Salisbury's letter as I have already described, and then shut up "the Lawn," put his servants upon board wages, and left them with the intimation that it would probably be many months before it was reinhabited. By that time, he argued, something definite would surely be arranged between him and his wife. He did not tell his mother and sisters, nor the ladies at Sorel Cottage, how Elfrida had left him, and why. He was naturally ashamed to confess that he had had no power to retain his young wife's affections, and that another man had won and cherished, under his very roof, what he had thought so lightly of, her heart. Perhaps, too, he was aided in this resolve, by some remnant of respect, for the feelings of the heart he had thus thrown away. I have no intention, at this crisis, of turning my sinner into a saint. A bad selfish man William Treherne had been from the beginning, and to the last day of his life, in some degree, a bad selfish man he will probably remain. But even bad men have some good traits about them, and selfish men are capable of feeling, and it is not a pleasant thing for even the worst of men to hear, that his wife has forgotten her marriage vow to love and cherish him, and has put it into effect instead, for the stranger sojourning within his gate. William Treherne had sinned, but he had also been sinned against. Elfrida acknowledged this throughout the darkest pages of her history. Why should I attempt to gloss over, or deny, what she confessed openly before God and man? Whatever his motives,

William Treherne did not betray his wife to his own relations. He told them, as soon as he knew it himself, that she had gone to make a long stay with her father in Scotland, nothing more. Her departure had been sudden; but, beyond that, nothing could be more natural than that she should visit Brackenburn. Her health had been delicate for some time, and the change would do her good. The Crossley Trehernes were not sufficiently interested in poor Elfrida to care to inquire further; and Agnes and her mother were too much occupied with their own cares, to leave them much time for speculating on other people's affairs. And so William Treherne bade farewell, for a while, to Milborough, and turned his footsteps towards London, where he had never failed yet of finding excitement to divert him from any phase of temperament. But the time seemed to hang heavily, even at his club. The season was at its height, but he was not an intellectual man to find pleasure in the glut of pursuits which might otherwise have attracted him, and married men, without their wives, are not in such request at evening parties, as not to leave many days upon their list of engagements, unfilled by invitations. And so, when one of William Treherne's most intimate friends, a brother civilian on leave from India, of the name of Pomfret, proposed to him that they should run over together to Paris for a few weeks, he accepted the offer with eagerness. It was of all things the one he should like best.

It was the very month for Paris. Paris was the only place worth calling a place, in the whole world. Hang London, and all its stupid so-called gaieties. Let us go at once! And so to Paris they went. But I do not think Mr. William Treherne enjoyed himself there so much as he had hoped to do. Generally, even since Ins marriage, he had seldom been at a loss for amusing himself. Low company, profligate companions, scenes of dissipation and unholy revelry, had never failed before to interest William Treherne, and to engage his attention. But

somehow, though Puris presented no lack of them, this time they failed. The sound of coarse language unrebuked, of indecent allusions from the mouths of women, of virtue ridiculed, and vice lightly spoken of, had lost their charm for him. They only brought back to his mind the remembrance of a woman from whom he had never heard any words, but such as were a fitting channel for the purity of her thoughts. For Elfrida was essentially fresh, innocent-minded and pure. They were the qualities which, combined with the beauty of her person, had first, if you remember, attracted him in her. For there is no doubt, that though whilst he considered her safely settled for life beneath his roof-tree, William Treherne had become worse than indifferent, towards his wife, now that she was virtually lost to him, he began, like a man, to dwell upon the virtues, and dream of the beauties, which, whilst they were common to him, he so neglected. It is the same with most of us; we never value anything so much as that which we cannot, or must not, have. The unattainable remains always fresh, because beyond our reach; and we often pass over the good we hold within our hands, to strain our vital energies in vain endeavours to reach that, which we know, if we could, we ought not to touch. William Treherne did not acknowledge to himself that he regretted the step he had driven Elfrida to take; he had not got so far as that; but the remembrance of ber would keep intruding itself when he least wished it to do so. Perhaps when he was listening to flatteries from some rosy lips, and watching the sparkle of the dark meretricious eyes which surmounted them, and wishing he could interest himself in what was being said, and admire what was being done, the pure pallor of Elfrida's face, the clear light of her liquid grey eyes, the shimmering sunshine on her golden hair, would rise up in succession upon his mental vision, and make the beauty before him, look coarse and artificial, beside the picture in his brain. Then perhaps when he was mixing in some scene of mirth and gaiety, and making a strong effort to mingle with

the rest and be gay, a little panorama of his quiet home life would appear before him, and shut out the intoxicating influences around him—only a recollection, perhaps, of a patient figure waiting for him to return to dinner, or bending over her work as she sat opposite to him during the evenings, or of a fair head laid back in troubled sleep on the pillow by his side—the eyelids stained with tears, the heart still throbbing, even in her dreams, under the influence of some unkind words spoken by himself. Very little to annoy a man, and yet enough to make him angry with himself, curt towards others, and distrait for the whole of the evening. Pomfret noticed his friend's moods, and mentioned them to him.

"You had better give up going out altogether, Treherne, if you can't make yourself more agreeable than that. Keally you positively affronted Mademoiselle de B last night by your rudeness and inattention., I never saw you in such a mood before. You'll lose your character for gallantry if you don't improve."

"I don't know what's come to myself, Pomfret," Treherne would answer. "Everything bores me, and to keep up one's attention to a lot of women chattering like magpies, is next to impossible. I'm sick of it all; I shan't go out any more."

"Shall you be moving homewards, then?" demanded his friend, presently.

"Not that I know of; why do you ask me?"

"Well, to tell you the truth, Stirling, whom I met last night, is just about to start upon a tour in Switzerland, with a young fellow of the name of Deschamps; and they rather wanted you and I to join them. They are going over the old ground again—Chamouni, the Tete Noir, Col de Balm, &c, and from thence, to cross the St. Bernard into Italy. I want to join them, but in your present state of turning up your nose at everything, I don't suppose you'd care to be of the party."

"Yes, I should," replied William Treherne; "it's just the thing I should like. I've been bothered and worried lately, and I want something to divert my mind. I've been too much used to the sort of life we've been living lately, for it to have any effect but boring me; but a walking tour is quite another thing. Climbing mountains, and changing the scene every hour, is just the kind of excitement I need. I shall be delighted to join you, Pomfret."

The gentleman he addressed, did not seem so delighted at the prospect as he was himself. William Treherne was too selfish a man to get on amongst men. Women gave in to him, and allowed him to have it all his own way, but he did not find men so complaisant; consequently, they often disagreed. And during the trip to Paris, he had come out in particularly unpleasant colours; so that Mr. Pomfret had rather congratulated himself upon the prospect of getting rid of his compagnon de voyage. But he was doomed to be disappointed; for William Treherne entered eagerly into all the preparations for the tour, and seemed the most interested of any of them in the route marked out for their pursuance. It was agreed that they were to start from Chamouni, attempt once more the ascent of Mont Blanc, in which they (that is, the projectors of the tour, Mr. Stirling, and his friend, Monsieur Deschamps), had already failed more than once; after which, they intended pursuing their route, as already described, by Mont St. Bernard into Italy; where such of their party as wished it, intended wintering. And so their plans were carried out, and the four men duly arrived at Chamouni, and had all things in readiness to attempt the ascent of the monarch of mountains, on the third day after they got there. Now I am not even going to try, to describe the manner, or means, by which they hoped to achieve an exploit which has been achieved by comparatively so few. In the first place, since Albert Smith made the ascent, every man, woman, and child, not only knows how it was done, but almost feels as if they had been there themselves; and in the second, as I have only ascended it myself, in company with that gentleman, and a numerous congregation of my fellow-creatures in the Egyptian Hall, I do not

feel in the least competent to bring forward any new ideas upon the subject. But as far as my four gentlemen are concerned, I must tell you that this last attempt proved the most miserable failure of the lot. They had found, on arriving at Chamouni, that the regular guides, the old-established family, who have conducted parties up the mountain for years past, were not to be procured; being away or engaged, or otherwise unattainable. And so, instead of waiting, impatient of delay, they tried the first who came to hand, or offered themselves for the purpose. Whether, therefore, they were unlucky in their guides, or the weather, or the time, I know not; but they were kept about such an unnecessary time, taken such a roundabout way, and, finally, found themselves surrounded, and overtopped, by such an apparently unscalable pyramid of glaciers, that, after a great deal of swearing at the guides, who did not understand half what they meant, and of useless gesticulation and argument between those individuals themselves, it was finally made known to the English gentlemen, by the interpretation of Monsieur Deschamps, that they were in, what is technically termed, "a regular fix," and the only thing to be done was, to turn back again, and try whether the descent of the mountain was easier than the ascent. Grumbling was of no use, neither was swearing; and as the four tourists were already very tired, very cold, and very hungry, they turned their steps again in the direction of Chamouni, with perhaps a better grace than they would otherwise have done. Each of the gentlemen was furnished with an alpenstock, and was also attached to a guide, by means of a rope; for although the descent of Mont Blanc is, perhaps, easier than the ascent, it is more dangerous. Mr. Stirling, Mr. Pomfret, and the young Frenchman, had all been up the mountain before, and knew a little of the risk attending negligence in obeying the directions of the guides; but William Treherne had not, and, added to his ignorance, he had an amount of obstinacy which prevented his accepting the constant cautions which were being given him, by the

men of his own party, as well as the guides, particularly his own, who kept on imploring him not to be so rash, and to trust more to him. But William Treherne was selfish into the bargain, and therefore the poor guide might as well have spared his warnings. He was quite a lad, the youngest of the party, and the terror he displayed, whenever his employer did anything rash, only incited Treherne on to further acts of foolhardiness; till, as they came to a place, where a glacier appeared to have cracked as it fell, leaving a fissure to be crossed, he met with the reward of his folly. He was about to leap the aperture, when Pomfret observed him.

"For God's sake, don't attempt that crevasse, Treherne; you might meet with your death."

"What, from that crack? why, I've jumped four times that width at home, standing."

"Yes, I dare say, from the dry ground; but it is very different landing on ice. You don't know how treacherous it is. Pray don't."

"Il ne faut pas que vous le faites, Monsieur Treherne; ce serait bien dangereux," said the Frenchman, in a tone of entreaty.

But William Treherne was evidently resolute in his intention.

"Don't be a fool, Treherne," said Pomfret, as he was carefully helped over the chasm himself, by means of a rope, and the assistance of two guides. "Let the guides haul you over, as they have us." But the only answer he got, was seeing Treherne plant his alpenstock on one side of the gaping fissure, whilst he prepared to swing himself over, as with a leaping pole, to the other. But he had forgotten the guide to whom he was securely attached, and the lad, instead of following him closely behind, alarmed at the rashness of the act, held back, and sealed both their fates by so doing; as the restraint made William Treherne lose his footing, as he came down upon the treacherous ice on the other side; and, with a sudden exclamation, followed by a scream from the lad, he fell backward, disappearing down the chasm, and dragging the unfortunate guide over with him as he fell. With a simultaneous burst of horror, mingled with not a few oaths, Englishmen and foreigners, alike rushed to the sides of the abyss, almost fearing they might never see anything of their unfortunate comrades again. But the calamity was not so great as they had anticipated. Far down beyond their reach, but not beyond the reach of their voices, William Treherne and his young guide had landed, unpleasantly enough, but still safely, upon a bed of snow.

"Holloa, Treherne," cried Pomfret, anxiously, "are you sure you are not hurt?"

"No, I'm not hurt; deuced long fall though, isn't it? How the devil I came to go down, I can't think; it must have been all this fool of a boy, that dragged me over."

"Is he hurt at all?"

"Don't know, I'm sure; he's groaning like anything. Can't you get us up? It's precious cold sitting on this snow, I can tell you."

"Oh, yes; we'll get you up directly, but don't you go leaping over any more chasms, now! you were warned often enough of the consequences: you're VOL. III. s lucky to get off with whole bones, I can tell you."

"I wish you'd hold your row," grumbled William Treherne, for it was his friend Pomfret who had been reviling him, "and make those fellows lower ropes or something, to land us out of this cursed hole, for we shall be frozen soon if you don't."

But when they came to put their desire into execution, it was found to be impracticable. There were no ropes long enough, or, if knotted together, strong enough, to bear the entire weight of such heavy bodies, as those of William Treherne, and the lusty young guide. By some negligence, fitting ropes for such a purpose had not been provided by the guides. They could be procured directly they reached Chamouni, but to make the attempt with their present ropes would be folly. They should only break them, perhaps hurt the gentleman by letting him fall again, and deprive themselves of the aid they afforded, without which

it was impossible they could surmount some of the difficulties which still lay before them before they reached the foot of the mountain.

"What's to be done, Treherne?' shouted Pomfret: "it seems to me, the only thing is for us to make our way down as quickly as we can, and send you up help. It is only two now, we shall reach Chamouni by four, and the guides will be back again by six. It's impossible we can haul you up with these ropes; they're far too slight."

"Why can't you try?" shouted William, in return.

"Because they would break, in all probability, and we should not even have the means of sending you back help. We should all be in the same fix. We will leave a guide by the chasm, that there may be no mistake about finding you, so you will be all right; and the sooner we go, the better for you. So good-bye, old fellow, and keep your spirits up."

"Good-bye," said Treherne, though sulkily; "it wasn't my fault this happened—it was all through this fool of a guide. Send back the fellows as soon as ever you can, for it's anything but warm here."

They threw him down their overcoats before they left, and all the brandy they could spare, reserving a very little for themselves in case of accident; and then they exhorted him to smoke hard, and drink little, till he was fetched away, and, whatever he did, not to go to sleep.

"I should think you had better pour a little of the liquor down that lad's throat," observed Pomfret, as he leant over the chasm to take a parting look at his friend; "he seems queer. Is he stunned, or what?" "Shaken a bit, I think," answered Treherne, as he turned over the body of the young guide, to examine it. He had not been so fortunate as himself; he had hit his head against the walls of the icy chasm as he fell, and was faint, and partially stunned by the blow. But after he had imbibed some of the brandy—to which generous liquor he was little accustomed—he opened his eyes, and sat up opposite to Treherne, whilst his comrade shouted to

him from above, and made him understand that aid was to be sent back for both of them. But as the day wore on, their situation became very difficult to bear with equanimity. The guide who had been left alone to mark the spot where they had fallen, was able to keep himself awake, and in something like life, by a little exercise. He was used to the mountain, and, narrow and slippery as his place for walking was, he still kept up a species of amateur patrol, through almost the whole of that long afternoon of waiting. But Treherne and his guide had no such means of alleviating their sensations of cold and drowsiness, nor of making the dreary moments of expectation go a little faster. They were afraid to move from their sitting position, having been especially warned not to do so by the guides; as, although they had happened to alight, in falling, upon a resting-place, there was no telling, through the treacherous snow, how far the foundation of it extended. So, further than placing the greatcoats and cloaks under them, though the snow had already penetrated through their clothing and made it quite wet, they did not stir from the position in which they had been left. William Treherne smoked until he could smoke no more, whilst the poor guide sat opposite to him, crouching down in the snow, upon the coat he had lent him, with his knees drawn up to his nose, and his elbows resting upon them. The long afternoon at last dragged itself away, and the night began to fall, and still no aid appeared. To William Treherne's continued inquiries to the guide above, the same answer was mechanically returned—

"Il n'y a rien encore en vue, monsieur." The darkness still continued to increase, and at last it was difficult for William Treherne to distinguish his companion opposite to him from the surrounding gloom; but still to all questions the mechanical answer came from the sentinel above— "Il n'y a rien encore en vue, monsieur."

At last, tired of waiting for the promised help, and beginning to feel a little alarmed at the uncomfortable turn, affairs seemed to be taking, William

Treherne began to talk to his young guide, for want of something better to raise his spirits.

"You seem low, my friend," he said, addressing him in French. "Cheer up! doubtless aid is near at hand by this time."

The patois in which the young man answered him was very difficult to understand, but William Treherne managed to make out, that his companion was suffering, not on account of fears for himself, but for the anxiety which some one at Chamouni would feel for his safety.

"She will weep, monsieur, and make herself ill, perhaps, with suspense and fear, and I would do much to save her from it."

"She—your mother, perhaps?"

"No, monsieur, not my mother; my wife."

William Treherne was surprised at the announcement, for his informant was a mere lad, of eighteen or nineteen perhaps, and looked even less than that.

"You many young in this country," he said. "We should consider you a mere boy in England."

"Should you, monsieur? I was eighteen last March. I cannot be too young to marry, since I am old enough to love."

"And have you never left this wife of yours for a night before, then?"

"Pardon, monsieur, yes; but not under such circumstances as these. The guides will tell her I have fallen, that is all, and she will imagine I am hurt— perhaps dead, before they reach the spot. And she is young, monsieur, young to bear pain."

"How old is she T demanded William Treherne.

"She is eighteen years and a half, monsieur—the same age as myself."

Eighteen years and a half! Just the age his wife had been when he married her!

"What is your name, lad?"

"Francois, monsieur."

"And your occupation?"

"Sometimes I work in the farm, sometimes I herd goats upon the mountains; at others, I go with visitors —as

I have with monsieur to-day—to show the road by which our guides reach the top. We are not rich, monsieur, and I must take what work I can—anything that will bring money to keep my Susette in food, and give her sometimes a new dress to deck her pretty figure. But I prefer home work to any other."

"Why?" asked William Treherne, mechanically.

"Does monsieur ask why, when he hears I have a young wife to look after, and to keep? Perhaps monsieur is not married yet, and does not know what a great charge marriage is. Susette is young, monsieur. She loves me; but she is very young, and she is pretty: and when a woman is both young and pretty, the men will tell her so. If I were to work away from Chamouni, and my Susette were to forget how much I love her, she might listen to the flatteries of others, and give them her heart instead of me. Not that she doesn't love me, monsieur," added the boy, eagerly, as if he were afraid Treherne might doubt his wife's faith to him. "Women will love any one who loves them; but she is young, and I cannot forget that it is a charge upon me, a great charge."

"It is a pity you took such a responsibility upon yourself so early," remarked his auditor.

"Oh, no, monsieur!" replied the lad; "it is a pleasure, for it takes little trouble to keep a woman's love; and there is nothing in the whole world that can compare with the happiness of possessing it. But hark, monsieur, I hear voices, and the sound of footsteps approaching! The guides are returning. Courage, monsieur; we shall soon be out of this hole."

This welcome intelligence was soon confirmed by the voice of the sentry above, who cried out—

"Courage, monsieur, les guides sont en vue. L'assistance est tout pres."

Then a few anxious moments passed, followed by the cheering sound of coming aid, and the blithe voice of Pomfret, who had insisted, tired as he was, upon returning with the guides to the assistance of his friend. Lanterns were soon lowered into the abyss, ropes knotted,

and thrown by a dozen strong hands; and when Treherne and the guide had mutually assisted in helping one another to fasten them round their bodies, the notice was given, and they slowly ascended the chasm, and soon found themselves upon the same spot from which they had fallen.

They commenced at once making the descent from the mountain, but with double caution, not only from the remembrance of their accident, but also because the presence of night rendered every step dangerous. But when William Treherne began to walk again, he found he had not escaped scot-free from his tumble, as he at first had imagined. Every bone ached, as he slowly dragged one foot before the other, in his downward journey; and every step becoming more painful, he was fully aware, long before they reached Chamouni, that he had at least been very violently contused from his sudden fall. But they did reach it at last, and it was with something very like a sigh of envy, that William Treherne saw the rough Francois welcomed, almost before he had gained the foot of the mountain, by the delighted Susette, who flew into his arms— a mass of demonstrative affection—a fresh, ordinary-looking, and rather clumsy Swiss peasant girl—nothing more! William Treherne thought of the face—the figure— that *ought* to have welcomed him from an accident which might have caused his death, and turned into the little hostelry of Chamouni, as if he wished to avoid the sight before him. But though dinner was ready and hot, awaiting him, he was feeling too ill to partake of it; and before the night was over, a little Swiss doctor had been sent for, from the neighbouring town, to see the Englishman who lay ill at Chamouni.

CHAPTER XHI. WILLIAM TREHERNE HAS TIME FOE THOUGHT.

The little Swiss doctor was not celebrated in his profession, but he knew enough about it to enable him to decide, that what the English gentleman was suffering from, was a violent contusion of the hip-bone, and that the pains he complained of were rheumatic, brought on by the exposure to cold, and the wet clothes he had sat in. Milord Treherne must rest himself in his bed for a few days, and undergo no further exertion, and doubtless all would be well; and the little Swiss doctor would have the pleasure of seeing him again on the following day. And so, leaving some innocent mixture for local application, he left William Treherne, groaning in his bed and cursing the folly which had brought him into such a plight. His three travelling companions left the little hostelry shortly after the doctor, and wandered about Chamouni and its environs all day, wondering how long it would be before Treherne was able to go on, and grumbling at the delay that his obstinacy had caused. At six o'clock they came back again to their dinner, still not in the best of tempers, particularly when they found the invalid was worse, instead of better, and they sat down to table in much the same state.

The wooden walls of the little hostelry were very thin and susceptible to sound, and the voices of the young men, excited over their subject, were eager and loud; consequently every word they uttered was plainly heard by William Treherne, who lay in the little room above where they were sitting; but for their credit I must say that they were not aware of the fact.

"What a deuced bore it is, this friend of yours falling ill, Pomfret," said Stirling, as the covers were removed. "If he goes and gets fever, or anything of that sort, I suppose he will spoil all our sport."

"Oh, no! you mustn't allow him to do it," was the answer. "You and Deschamps must go on as you at first intended, and I will stop here till he is able to travel, and then we can catch you up. It's an awful sell, but it can't be helped."

"It could have been helped very well, if it had not been for Treherne's deuced folly. You must excuse me, Pomfret, but I can't say I like your friend."

Pomfret laughed.

"Don't call him a friend of mine. I know him well enough, because we were living close together for some time

in India; but Treherne is a man that the more you know of the less you are likely to call a friend."

"So I should think," rejoined the first speaker.

"Who is he; one of General Treherne's sons?"

"No; his father was a private gentleman, I believe, living at Milborough. This fellow came into a tidy lot of money when the old gentleman kicked. Married one of Dr. Salisbury's daughters, of Madras, no end of a fine girl."

"What, is he married?" said Stirling.

"Monsieur Treherne marie?" exclaimed the Frenchman, who could understand English, although he could not speak it. "C'est incroyable! Il parle toujours comme un garcon, meme comme un celibataire tres libre."

"Well, he is then, and no mistake about it. I've seen his wife several times. She has been a very pretty woman, but she looks awfully sick and downey. They say he's a regular brute to her."

"Just what I should have expected of him," said Stirling. "He has no mercy on animals, and can't speak civilly to a servant; and those are just the fellows who ill-treat women."

"Yes; and I can't understand it; for she seemed such a quiet kind of girl, quite young, you know, and looking as innocent as a sucking-dove. I dare say she gives in to him in everything. Treherne ought to have caught a regular Tartar; that would have done him good!"

"Ah; that would have taught him not to be always thinking of himself, and never of any one else. I think his selfishness is disgusting. Well, if he doesn't use his wife well, I hope somebody will relieve him of the trouble of her. If you'll give me a letter of introduction, Pomfret, I'll try what I can do when I get home again."

William Treherne ground his teeth together as he listened to the careless talk of the young Englishmen, and thought how he had laid himself and his wife open to be discussed, and commented upon. The truth brought home to him thus roughly, from other lips,

was doing more towards opening his eyes to his own past conduct, than any advice or counsel, however kindly meant, could have done. As he lay there, thinking on the words he had heard, the conversation he had held with the young guide in the snowy chasm recurred to his memory. Was he to be taught his duty by a peasant boy, and a lot of careless young bachelors? But the conversation was still going on, and he settled himself again to listen.

"I don't see, Pomfret," said the voice of Stirling, "why you should have your lark spoilt altogether, for that selfish brute upstairs. We didn't want him to come with us at the commencement, and he has been nothing but a nuisance all along, never choosing to accommodate himself to anything. Leave him to the doctor and the landlord here, they'll look after him well enough, and you come along with us. If we don't start soon, we shall have the summer over before we reach the end of our journey, and we don't want that."

"If I didn't think it would prove anything serious," began Pomfret

"Why, man alive! what a fuss you make about the fellow. If it is serious, serve him right, I say, for being so obstinate and stuck-up. For my part, I think a few weeks of bed and rheumatism, would do him no end of good—give him time for repentance." And Stirling burst out laughing, in which he was joined by Monsieur Deschamps.

"That wouldn't do any of us harm, I dare say," returned Pomfret, without joining in the laugh; "but I should scarcely feel comfortable in leaving him here alone. Other men might make friends among strangers, but Treherne manages to be so universally disliked."

A pleasant truth for the sick man to hear! It seemed as though he could bear it no longer, for he turned round in his bed with his face towards the wall, and drew the clothes about his ears, to shut out the sound of the voices below; but no more was said that could have given him pain.

"Let us wait until to-morrow," added Pomfret, "and hear what the doctor says, before we decide upon anything definite."

When the doctor came on the morrow, he found his patient feverish, but otherwise not worse. "How long would it be before Milord Treherne would be capable of resuming his interesting journey? oh, in a week, certainly a week. The rest and quiet of that time would set milord up again, and he would be well and strong as ever." But the prospect of a week spent in Chamouni, where there is nothing to do, see, or think about, was a serious consideration to the energetic young men who had asked the question of the old Swiss doctor. What might they not do in a week? They certainly must go on, and Treherne could join them, by rail or diligence, as soon as he was well, easily enough. He would lose part of the tour, but it was his own fault, and he must pay for his whistle. So it was decided, by Stirling and the young Frenchman, but Pomfret still held back—he would like to go on with them, and yet he could not bear the idea of leaving a sick friend alone. He was a kind, generous fellow, was Mr. Pomfret, and possessed the true nobility we find in so many English hearts, that can forget past annoyance and present trouble, in the time of need. He would not agree to start with his companions, at all events until he had spoken with Treherne; and he entered that gentleman's bedroom with the full determination of telling him, that he had decided to stay behind and nurse him, until he was well enough to resume the walking tour. But William Treherne was in an unfortunate humour for accepting an obligation. What he had overheard his companions say at the dinner-table, had made him take a dislike to all of them, and particularly to Pomfret, whom he had considered his friend. VOL. III. T

He felt sure that what they said was true—something in his heart had told him so at the time, and returned often afterwards to remind him of the unpleasant fact; and that, combined with the pain he was suffering—for William Treherne had never been gifted with much fortitude for bearing any inconvenience— had considerably aggravated the usual ill-temper that he displayed, under anything that was not pleasant.

"Well, Treherne," said Pomfret's cheerful voice, as he seated himself near the bed, "how do you feel to-day?"

"You can see I'm no better," was the peevish answer.

"These fellows want to continue their tour, and let us catch them up, as soon as you are able to travel. The doctor says you will be all right in a week; they wouldn't have got very far by that. time. What do you say to it?"

"I say, let them go—to the devil, if they like." "Not quite so far as that, I hope," said Pomfret, laughing, "particularly as we are to follow them. We shall pick them up probably at Martigny, at the slow rate they travel"

"I shall probably not pick them up at all," grumbled Treherne. "I shall go back to Paris after this bout, or perhaps home."

"To Paris!" exclaimed Pomfret. "Oh! I hope not. I thought you took such an interest in this tour, and enjoyed it."

"No, I don't a bit."

"Oh! I say; this is a sell," said Pomfret, ruefully.

"What difference can it make to you?" demanded Treherne.

"Why, of course it does, as I am going to stay with you, Treherne. I shall not only lose a week's touring, but I shall have to rejoin them alone. I made sure you would come."

"I don't want you to stay with me," said Treherne, rudely. "I never asked you. I shall do well enough alone—indeed, better. You fellows make a confounded row when you're in the house, and it's enough to drive a man mad when he's ill."

"But who will there be to talk to you, and keep you company if I go? You will want more than mere waiting on, Treherne."

"No, I shan't. I don't want company. I'd rather be without it."

Pomfret was piqued at the indifference he dis played to the sacrifice he had intended making for him, and told him so.

"In that case," he said, "it's no use my stopping. I can't say you are particular-ly grateful, Treherne, and I dare say if I had remained, I should have got more kicks than halfpence for my pains. Still, if you change your mind before to-morrow, let me know."

The delight of Stirling and Deschamps at hearing Treherne did not intend rejoining them was great.

"Deuced good riddance," said Stirling, with his usual energy. "Now we'll have something like fun. Pomfret, we start at five o'clock to-morrow morning. I declare I feel just like a donkey that's kicked its panniers off."

"C'est un grand soulagement," exclaimed Monsieur Deschamps; "il est prudent de reflchir deux fois, avant d'inviter un Stranger a se joindre a nos fines parties."

Still the kind-hearted Pomfret had his generous scruples, and it was with a face of concern that he asked William Treherne the next morning, before they started, if there was nothing he could do for him—no letter to be written, or comforts procured.

"Nothing, thank you," was the surly answer. "I shall be twice as comfortable when you are all gone."

And so Pomfret left Chamouni with his friends, though not without many injunctions to the landlord of the hostelry, to see that every attention was paid to the sick Englishman left in his care. And every attention was paid that could be. The little Swiss doctor attended him regularly, and the innocent lotions were rubbed in without any effect, and the innocent potions poured down his throat by the gallon, and yet he grew no better. The pains he had complained of, increased and multiplied, until there was not a part of his whole body that was not racked with agony; and with it came the fever— strong and continuous, which abated a little towards morning, comparatively disappeared after breakfast-time, increased with the dinner hour, and raged towards night, often flying to his head and making him delirious. The fact is, he had caught a severe attack of rheumatic fever, and the best physician in the world could only have cured him by dint of time. As it was, under the unsophisticated hands of the little Swiss doctor, he bid fair to succumb to it altogether. The agonising pain he suffered was greatly

N aggravated by his incapability of making the honest, but coarse, Swiss peasants understand the elegant Parisian French which he spoke. By their rough handling and clumsy attentions, they greatly increased the pain he felt. Sometimes it was almost beyond bearing; and his blood-shot eyes and drawn, lengthened features, testified to the great suffering he was called upon to bear, during those long and lonely weeks of sickness. During those miserable hours, the conversation he had overheard from the companions of his journey rankled in his mind. Had he, then, made himself so utterly disagreeable to all his friends? If they had perceived it, even those strangers, who had only met him under circumstances of enjoyment, how much more must it have been felt by those, who knew him intimately? Had he treated Elfrida like a brute? Something whispered to him that he had. It was in vain he tried to excuse himself, upon the plea that she had been faithless to him—at least in heart. He had not known of her faithlessness then; he had had no idea of it. Could he have driven her by neglect to love another? As the idea flashed on the wretched man's mind, he groaned. What was it the young guide had said?—" She is young and pretty, and when a woman is both, the men will tell her so." "Marriage is a great charge; I feel it to be so." "Women will love any one who loves them." "It is little trouble to keep, and there is no happiness like the possession of a woman's love. " Who was,he speaking of—Susette or Elfrida? himself or William Treherne? He could hardly remember, he was so weak. But a woman's love—if a woman really loved one—it must be a great happiness; almost worth being ill to be nursed by such. How soft her hands used to be! how doubly soft her cheeks! and he sighed, as he thought what it would be, to feel that soft hand and cheek against his burning head. But she had loved George Treherne, not him; she would have gone to him if he had been sick. William Treherne did not

suppose she would come to him, even if he asked her. Her last words were in his ears—" He left me, as I preferred to be left, to virtue and misery." Misery! had he really made her, then, so wretched? He turned the matter over and over in his mind, and could come to no conclusion. He supposed it must be so; Pomfret said that others had observed it. If it was the common talk, he supposed it must be true. But he was sorry now he had written that letter to her father. As the thought of the allowance he had offered his wife came into his head, he blushed. "I wonder if she thought I wished to insult her," he said to himself. "I didn't though, but I was very angry; and justly so. I can, at all events, write and retract my letter so far. We shall never live together again; but she must have a fitting allowance for her station, and mine. I wonder if women ever love a second time: I have loved several times in my lifetime. I wonder if they forget easily, or if "And here his meditations would be interrupted, perhaps, by a series of groans, as the dreadful pains of rheumatic fever came back upon him, and made him feel as if he was on the rack. He grew weaker every day, his appetite had failed, his hands and feet were crippled, and even the mild remedies suggested by the Swiss doctor being generally only half applied by the ignorant Swiss servants, to whom (by reason of his swearing and impatience) the English gentleman was an object of great fear, there seemed little prospect of an amendment. William Treherne felt himself that he was daily growing worse. Sometimes now, he was quite unable to think, or to reason, and his longing to have some of his own country-people near him— some woman to nurse him—resolved itself at last into a constant craving. The form of Elfrida, so light and sylph-like, would flit before his eyes, until he could have declared that she had been in the room. He would dream of her soft, cool hands upon his brow, of her fresh lips pressed to his, her quiet eyes looking into his own, and would wake, burning with fever, groaning with pain, and ready to swear at every one who dared to approach him,

and convince him of the cruel reality, that he was away from home, sick, unattended, unloved, and uncared for. If he had known where to address to his friend Pomfret, he would even have pocketed his pride, and written to ask him to overlook his past rudeness, and come back to him; and Pomfret would have obeyed the call; but he was wandering about—here one day and there the next—and had left no address by which Treherne could be sure of a letter reaching him. And still his longing for a familiar face increased more and more. "I wonder if my mother or Dora would come to me," he thought. "I must have somebody. I don't believe I shall ever get up again. I can t die like a dog, alone."

For the great depression of spirits which forms a characteristic of his disease, lost none of its force upon a temperament like William Treherne's. But his hands were too crippled to hold a pen, and his head almost too weak to form a sentence. He was entirely dependent on the little Swiss doctor for communicating with his friends; but the doctor was delighted to make himself useful, and brought the letter, written to inform Mrs. Treherne of her son's illness, the next day to his patient, that he might dictate the address to him.

"A Madame—Madame William Treherne,—et comment appellez-vous l'addresse, monsieur?"

William Treherne's aching head tried to remember the name of Crossley, in vam. Then he thought Milborough would do, knowing that his wife was at Brackenburn, and too weak to think of the probable consequences of sending it there. And so, after a great deal of explanation, relative to the spelling of the words, " Milborough, Hampshire," was transcribed on the envelope, and the letter was posted the same afternoon. At Milborough it arrived in due course, and the postman, knowing there was but one "Mrs. William Treherne" in Milborough, took it to the Lawn; and there, the servants, supposing of course that it was for their mistress, redirected it to Brackenburn, as they had been ordered to do with all letters that might arrive, and it reached Elfrida on the third day after it had been written; and though I have not detailed the time, this was just about, where we last left her, at the Hermitage, three months after the death of Helene Treherne. The letter reached her early one morning, and she opened it, imagining of course that it was for her. The little doctor's writing was very peculiar, and that, added to the foreign language, made her slow in deciphering its meaning. It was a brief note, merely stating that Monsieur Treherne had been lying ill of rheumatic fever, for some weeks, at Chamouni, and was very desirous of the presence of his mother or sister, as he was low in spirits—a state of things dependent upon the nature of his complaint. When Elfrida had read it, and found it was intended for her mother-in-law, instead of herself, she handed the letter to Grace, saying—

"I must forward that to Crossley at once, Grace, I suppose."

But when Grace had read it also, she held a different opinion from her sister.

"I should not forward it at all, Elfrida, if I were you."

"Not forward it, when it is addressed to her! Why, what else could I do?"

"Go to William yourself."

"Grace!"

"Yes, Elfrida. It is no use saying 'Grace!' and looking at me in that manner. You know what my opinion has been all along. This letter has come to you by accident, but it ought to have done so by rights. You are the proper person to nurse your husband. Go to him at once."

"But, Grace," faltered Elfrida, "he has not asked for me; he asked for his mother or sister. He does not want me!"

"How can you tell, Elfrida? You read, he is low in spirits; perhaps it is this very separation that makes him so."

"He said one roof should never cover us again, for ever."

"Yes, when he was angry with you, and, Elfrida, can you say, not justly so? Now he is sick, and in need of tender nursing; and even if he has not asked for you, your duty is to go. H he turned you out of doors again, Elfrida, you would be happier than if you stayed here. You

know what your duty is, my dear, you have acknowledged it often of late. Don't let me think you said what you did not mean."

Still Elfrida was irresolute.

"I know it would be my duty to live with him again, if he asked me, Grace; but to go to him unasked—to risk having the confession I made to him thrown in my teeth—perhaps to hear that name reviled again—oh! I could not!" And Elfrida shuddered at the idea.

"Elfrida, my dear sister, what are you living for? What is your chief hope T

She turned round quickly—

"Oh, Grace, you know. Heaven!"

"How do you expect to get there, my dear? By shirking what you know to be your duty, or by walking in the plain path set before you? Elfrida, it is only by sacrificing your inclinations to what is right, that you will ever get there. Besides, I will not believe that in this instance, your inclinations do not go hand in hand with your duty. It is your pride, Elfrida, that is keeping you back. Think of your poor husband, in that dreadful pain and weakness, in a foreign country, with no one to nurse him. Frida, he might die j what then T

She was subdued now, and her tears commenced falling.

"I will go, dear Grace," she said; "you always set me right. I have resolved, by God's help, to do my duty, and it is plain enough. I will go, for your sake and his."

And so the letter was never forwarded to Mrs. Treherne of Crossley; but her daughter-in-law wrote to her instead, to say that she had received news that her husband was lying ill in Switzerland, and she was about to set out on the morrow to join him. But Dr. Salisbury would not let her go alone. She was too young to travel by herself, and he was not quite certain of what kind of welcome she might receive at her husband's hands, though he did not hint anything of the kind to her.

You will need my protection, dear child, as far as Chamouni; and if your husband is desirous of moving from there, before he is quite convalescent, you will want my help then. Besides, I trust I may be

of use to him in his illness."

And so they made all arrangements for starting on the morrow.

When it arrived, and Elfrida descended to the breakfast-room ready for her journey, Grace was surprised to see that the mourning she had worn for the last three months, was laid aside, and that she was in colours again. Elfrida noticed her astonishment at once—

"I thought it best, dear," she said, in answer to her sister's look; "it can make no real difference; and you know William dislikes black so much. I thought it might worry him perhaps and remind him of—of—past things! Oh, Grace, darling!" she added, in a burst of fervour, "you have taken a great deal of trouble with me, in teaching me my duty, and I will not do it by halves. Whilst I was putting on my coloured things this morning, I could not help thinking, for the first time, that what you have said all along, may really be coming tme, and they seemed like the omens of something brighter for me in the future. Grace, dear, perhaps things may come right after all—who knows!" CHAPTER XIV.

PEACE BETWEEN THEM.

Aftee William Treherne was aware that the letter which the doctor had written to inform his mother of his illness had been actually despatched, he became very restless. Not that any affection subsisted between himself and his own family; on the contrary, they were as indifferent towards one another, as mother and children, and brothers and sisters, could well be; but the man was utterly prostrate in mind and body, and he thirsted for the sight of a well-known face—for some one to speak to in his own language, and of his own affairs. For there was springing up in his heart, day by day, a rapidly increasing desire to hear news of Elfrida—to hear of her health and her doings—to glean, if possible, some knowledge of her thoughts concerning the past, and of her feelings in the present. For now he had lost her, he began to see, not what she had been, but what she might have been to him, had he so chosen it. Looking back upon the last two years, as he lay through some of those sleepless nights, afraid to move for pain, he could not remember any time, excepting perhaps during the first few weeks of his married life, in which he had made his wife his companion. As soon as they had reached England, he had followed his own pursuits, revelled in his own pleasures, neither of which were such, as married men usually indulge in; and had thought it quite sufficient if his wife had his house to live in during his absence, his horses to use, and his money to spend. He had always thought her too childish to consult about any of his private affairs; he had treated her as a child, without ever taking the trouble to find out, whether she was so, or not. She was so young—she had looked so simple, so innocent, so child-like. All these were the very things he had thought so charming, when he first saw her. His memory flew back to the picture she had presented the day they had spent together at Malta — the picture of youth, and health and beauty; and then he compared it with what she was now—thin, pale, wasted, and sadlooking. Where were the mad spirits, that used to make prudish matrons shake their heads over her to VOL. III. u express their disapproval?—where the ringing peals of laughter, so joyous and so infectious, that those who heard them could not but join in her merriment? Gone—all gone, with her looks of childlike purity. And what had stolen them from her? The love of George Treherne? No! Her husband could remember that she had begun to fade before that time. Her fading had commenced with her married life. She had confessed from the first that she did not care for him, and yet he had taken no pains to win her love—no pains to keep her out of the way of those, who might try to win it. How she must have suffered, before he wrung the fatal confession from her that had parted them. He could look back now on her frequent illnesses, her despondency, her quiet resignation, one by one, of all her merry girlish tricks, her arch fun, her half-shy, halfimpertinent badinage; and in exchange for them, remember the patient submission, the meek answers,.

which he had so often received, in return for harsh commands and unkind words. And through it all, she had borne that sad secret about with her, which must indeed have become a burden, before she would have trusted it to the care of so hard a taskmaster as he had made himself to her. And yet she had stayed by him. She might have left him, but she had stayed. For William Treherne believed fully in his wife's truth towards him. He knew she did not love him, but he was sure of his own honour. She was too pure, too good, too true (even to him), for that. But he had let her heart slip away from him; he had let another man win what he had cared so little (or thought he cared so little) about. But now that it was gone—that it could never be his, he knew that he did care. "Oh, if I could only hive the past two years over again!" he would sigh to himself as he thought thus. "What a number of women I have known, and trifled with, and thought I loved, in my lifetime; but now that I am so near death, there is not one I would care to see at my bedside, but the woman who belongs by right to myself; and of all the women in the world, she seems the least attainable to me!"

What would he have thought, could he have known that at that very moment, she was travelling as fast a3 she could towards him!

On the evening on which she and her father reached Chamouni, William Treherne was very ill. The Swiss doctor, not finding his innocuous lotions and potions take the effect he hoped, had tried bleeding his patient, and had weakened him in consequence to a frightful extent. So much so, that as the day drew on, and no news came, by post or otherwise, of the approach of the relations he looked for, Treherne gave up the hope of seeing any of his own people again, for he fully expected he should not last out the night. But weak as he was, he could not sleep; and the unusual bustle, late in the evening, of an arrival at the little hostelry could not but attract his notice. He heard at once that some one had come, and for him; and became, in consequence, as greatly ex-

cited as his state would permit him to be. Dr. Salisbury and his daughter were met, on their entering the sitting-room of the hostelry, by the little doctor, who commenced, in his strange patois, and with much gesture, to explain to them, that his patient was going on as well as possible. But he was interrupted by the servant who had been left in attendance upon Treherne, entering to say, that "milord" wished to see the lady at once, as he was very impatient. The little doctor turned round to Elfrida, with an intimation that he would show her the way up-stairs. If he imagined she was the mother of his patient, to whom he had written, he must certainly have thought that she was a very young one. But Elfrida guessed his intention of accompanying her, and turned to her father for relief—

"Alone, papa, please!"

Then Dr. Salisbury informed the doctor, that the lady was Mr. Treherne's wife, and that she desired to go up-stairs by herself; and the little man only bowed her out of the room in consequence.

She did not feel nervous or excited. If she had loved this man, meeting him again, after the circumstances under which they had parted, would have agitated her to a fearful extent; but for Elfrida, all violent feeling seemed to be past. There is a climax in this life, both in mental and bodily pain, after which we can feel no more, and after it, all other sources of emotion appear tame in comparison; and this climax Elfrida had gone through, and done with.

As she turned the handle of the bedroom door, she neither hesitated nor trembled, but walked straight in. Yet she had some feeling left, for when the sick man's eyes—which had been turned, greedy with expectation, towards the entrance—fell on her figure, and he closed them hastily, saying, "Elfrida, who sent you here?" she stood where she was, without advancing further, bitterly disappointed. Pre sently she said, in a low voice, "William, don't you want me? Shall I go back again?" Then he opened his eyes again, and answered quickly and eagerly, "No, no!

Elfrida, come to me. I have *longed* for you." And as she went forward, and, kneeling by the bedside, put her arm about his wasted neck and shoulders, and stroked his crippled hand in hers, the man, weakened by illness, humbled by a review of his past life, and touched to the quick by his wife's voluntary return to him, burst into tears upon her bosom. It is a dreadful thing to see a man cry—any man, even if it is not one we love; and Elfrida was a woman, full of all womanly compassion and regret for the poor sick creature who lay in her arms. So no wonder, that, in that moment, her tears mingled freely with his, and she was ready to take all the blame of their wretched married life upon herself. Presently Elfrida whispered, as she wiped away the tears which were streaming down his cheeks— William, papa is here. He came with me to see if he can do you any good. I did not know you were ill, or I should have come before. Now I have come, you will soon be well again I hope, and then we will all go home together."

"Who told you I wanted you *T* he said.

"No one, dear. The doctor's letter to your mother was sent on to me by mistake, and I came directly. I knew you would want me. Now let me go and call papa, for he is anxious to see you."

So she left him to tell her father. Her simple—

"Papa, it is all right; William is very glad to have us here," told Dr. Salisbury all he wished to know, and he accompanied her up-stairs to see the sick man. William Treherne looked very much ashamed of himself, through all his weakness, as his father-in-law entered the room, but Dr. Salisbury was too kind not to set any one at ease, who felt awkward in his presence. He found, on inquiry, that he had been miserably treated by the Swiss doctor, who had well-nigh killed him; first by neglect, and then by too violent remedies. But it had been meant in kindness, and so Dr. Salisbury would not take the case out of his hands. He only professed to consult with him upon the best means of treating Treherne, and during the con-

sultation, managed to get his own way in everything. The treatment was completely changed. Late as it was, messengers were despatched to Martigny, for such drugs as Dr. Salisbury had been unable to bring with him, and such as he had were immediately put into requisition. Hot fomentations and baths, in which were infused wonderful chemicals, which soothed the racking pain, and tended to unstiffen the poor contracted joints, were prepared and used at once, and proved highly beneficial. The two doctors managed to lift poor Treherne out of his bed without further assistance; but he would not let his wife leave his side. Once, as he was being moved for some purpose, which compelled them to put him to great pain, it was almost too much for him, and as he was placed in the chair, his features worked with the agony he was feeling. His head was resting upon Elfrida's shoulder at the time, and the poor wasted contracted face was brought close to hers. As he winced under the suffering, she pressed her lips to his, and said "My poor husband." The action and the words seemed to revive him, he opened his eyes, tried to lay his crippled hand about her neck, and fainted in the attempt. But when the bath had been allowed a fair trial, and he was put back into bed again, he felt so much soothed by the remedies that had been used, that he fell asleep, a luxury he had not enjoyed for many days past, with his hand fast locked in Elfrida's. As soon as she was sure that he was really slumbering, she disengaged it as gently as she could, and went down to join her father, at the meal which had been prepared for them; for they had not broken their fast for several hours. They were alone, the Swiss doctor, finding his patient was in such good hands, having gone home. Elfrida sat for some time in silence, but then she said timidly—

"Papa, dear."

"Well, darling," was Dr. Salisbury's answer.

"You remember the story of my married life as I told it you at Brackenburn."

"I am not likely to forget it, Elfrida."

"I know that," she answered; "but I want you to try and forget it, papa—or, at least, to live and act as if you had never heard it. It was quite true, and it is very sad, but perhaps I was wrong to make it as public as I did. It was a comfort to me to talk of my great grief, and I did not think of the conse, quences. But now that William seems so glad to have me back again, perhaps—he may love me again, papa," she said, almost interrogatively.

"It is strange if he doesn't, my child," was her father's answer.

"Oh! but papa, I was very wrong; I made him very angry, and I can see it all now. I do not know, if the time came over again, but that I should act the same. I cannot tell;.but I can see how wrong I was. The sorrow remains the same, and it will always remain so— but so will the wrong. Papa, I shall never forget George!" and she swallowed a sob as she spoke; "but if William wishes me to live with him again, I must try and forget all my past married life, and begin afresh. And I want you to promise me that you'll help me, by trying to forget it too; and then, perhaps, the task will be easier. Don't ever speak to me of it, papa, dear; don't allude to it in any way, and I may, perhaps, come some day to forget that it has ever been."

But her looks belied the words she spoke. Dr. Salisbury readily gave the desired promise, and urged his daughter retiring to the rest she so much needed. But she expressed her intention of taking the servant's place by her husband's side.

"I came here to nurse him, papa," she said, "and he will want me at night, more than any other time." And so each time the sick man woke, he still saw, by the light of the night-lamp, that slight dressing-gowned figure sitting by his side, half asleep perhaps, tired as she was by travelling, but always ready to hand him his medicine, or the beverage provided for his drinking, or to moisten his hot head and hands with vinegar and water, until, refreshed again, he once more sank off to sleep. He was too weak to thank her much, too drowsy almost from the sedative Dr. Salisbury had administered to him, even to notice her, but he knew she was there, and that she was Elfrida, and his grateful eyes thanked her when he uttered no words. How thankful she was as she watched beside him, through that first night, to think that she had taken Grace's advice, and come. How grateful to God, that He had so wonderfully crowned her effort to do right, by such an unmerited reward. For Elfrida could not yet think of herself without the greatest humility. The next afternoon William Treherne was much better. There is no doubt that his mind being set at rest respecting his wife, had a great deal to do with it; but Dr. Salisbury, of course, took all the credit to himself. The patient was so much freer from pain, that his father-in-law proposed leaving him, to make a little excursion into the country, for the ostensible reason of procuring him fruit. Of course Elfrida would not leave the sick-room, and so she and her husband were left alone together. It was almost for the first time, for Dr. Salisbury had not left his son-in-law for more than ten minutes at a time, during the entire morning. Elfrida had no work at hand, and so she took a book she had been reading during her journey, with the intention of finishing it, and sat herself down upon the floor, with her head resting against the side of the low bed on which her husband lay. It was not long before his hand found its way amid the masses of her fair hair, and rested there caressingly—but still she read on. But a sudden pressure on her head made her look round, and then he said earnestly—

"Elfrida, why don't you reproach me?"

"Keproach you, William!" she said; "for what?"

"For my unkindness to you—my brutality. I drove you from my house; but I didn't half mean what I said, Elfrida. I hardly expected you would take me at my word."

"Oh, William!" she exclaimed, throwing down her book upon the floor, as she rose and knelt besidi him, "it is I who ought to ask you to forgive me. I do not wonder now, that you were angry with me; but it was my great sus-

pense and grief, that forced my secret from me. Can you forget it? Can you, I mean," she said, whilst the blushes mantled fast upon her cheek, "try to forget that I ever told it you? Our married life has been a sad mistake, William; perhaps it was my fault; 1 was too young to marry, and you did not look after me enough, and left me too much with your cousin, and so I came to love him. Oh! William, don't look like that," she said, as her husband's eyelids drooped beneath her words. "I could not speak to you of it, if he were still with us; but God has put an end to it for ever. I have done you a grievous wrong, William, but I have suffered for it very bitterly; will you forgive me, and let me try to begin my life anew? I think I could do better if I tried; I am sure I could do better if you loved me."

His only answer was to fold his arms about her neck, and kiss the golden crown which was bowed down before him.

"Elfrida," he said, presently, "my dear child, we have wronged each other; but I have been the worst of the two. I see, now, that if you had left me for another's protection, the fault could" only have been laid at my own door."

"Oh, no! William," she replied; "don't say that."

"I feel it," he said; "you are a child compared to me, and I have left my child too much to herself.

But, as you say, God has swept away the obstacles to our future happiness by opening both our eyes, and making me feel, by this severe illness, how necessary my wife is to me. Let us forgive each other, Frida, and try to forget the past, in the future."

She sealed the compact with a kiss, but she returned to her book with a sigh, which, though unheard, came from her very heart. It was easier for him to forget, than for her. As the days went on, and he grew better, and required no more nightwatching, she had a bed made up for herself, by his request, in his room. Then it was, as sometimes lying awake himself, he watched her restless slumbers, he found that it is not a kiss, and a few words of kindness, that

can wipe out the remembrance of a bitter past, or undo the work of years. As her fancy —always excitable and nervous—wandered in dreams of the past, Elfrida's lips would give vent to her thoughts, and sometimes the name of her lover would break from her, and make the unfortunate husband re-echo the heavy sighs which accompanied it. Sometimes, he would be aroused himself from sleep by her exclamations of horror at some sudden discovery, or plaintive entreaties to some person or persons unknown, to give her back her child; or prayers to the absent man, now far away in India, to go and leave her, only to leave her, before she died. Not pleasant words for a husband to hear, even when the sad circumstances are known to him; and poor William Treherne used to turn groaning on his bed when they reached his ears, and felt at such times that the punishment of his neglect of his wife was harder than he deserved. But by day, nothing could exceed her kindness and attention to himself, and once, when he was alluding to her restlessness by night, something of the truth flashed on her mind, and she blushed deeply.

"William," she said, "let me have my bed removed into-another room. I disturb you, I am sure."

"No," he said, gloomily; "I'm getting used to it." But there was pain in his voice, and she noticed it.

"If I dream more by night, dear," she whispered, "it is because I think less by day. William, I am happier than I was. Don't you believe it T

And he would have been an infidel indeed, if he had not believed in the truth of the honest eyes which met his own as she asked the question.

He told himself that he did not mind it; that of course he knew she had cared for the man, and he supposed it would be some time before she forgot him again. And yet one night, some weeks afterwards, when she began to toss and tumble about, as she usually did, preparatory to talking in her sleep, and he, being awake, resolved that, whatever she said, he would try and not think of it afterwards, something fell from her lips which made William Treherne start up in his own bed, with a flush on his cheek, and a glad light in his eyes, which had never displayed itself before at anything she had said. And yet they were only a few words, only an entreaty to be believed.

"I do love you," she had murmured rapidly, as sleepwakers will; "I do love you, indeed I do; don't you believe me, William?"

He had not credited that he could have heard the last word aright, but, as he listened breathlessly, she repeated it.

"Don't you believe me, William?" And then he had crept out of his bed, and bending over her, had kissed her in her sleep, until he had roused her, and she scolded him for being out of bed, for the nights were getting chilly, and he was yet far from strong. And he had gone back again to his couch, and fallen asleep with a happy smile upon his lips, and that sentence ringing in his ears like a blessed lullaby.

This had been the night before Dr. Salisbury was to leave them to return to England. He had been three or four weeks at Chamouni now, and William Treherne-was convalescent, and quite able to be left to his wife's care, until they could travel together. Before they parted, it was agreed that as soon as the Trehernes reached England again, they were to visit Brackenburn at once, and spend Christmas with the Salisburys; for they did not intend to leave the Continent directly. William was still an invalid, and would be for some time, and Elfrida had never been there before, and was anxious to see more of it. Therefore, as soon as he was able, her husband proposed to take her on to Italy, which would still leave them time to reach Brackenburn by Christmas; at which period, Douglas Cameron, it was expected, would have arrived in England, to add another to the family group. As William Treherne wrung the Doctor's hand at parting, the latter said, playfully

"Take care of my girl, Treherne."

But his son-in-law answered him seriously—

"You are not afraid to trust her to me now, are VOL. III. X you, sir? You need not be, I will guard her with my life."

"No! my dear William, I am not," was the father's reply; "nor afraid to trust you with her, for your mutual happiness is in one another's hands. God bless you both!"

That evening, as the husband and wife sat together over their cosy supper-meal, in the little sitting-room of the hostelry, William drew Elfrida to his side, and asked her if she meant the words she had used the night before in her sleep.

"What words?" she said, with an unconscious air. Then he repeated them to her, and she blushed as if she had been detected in a fault.

"Are they true, Elfrida?" he said, entreatingly. 'Tell me, darling."

Then she answered him at once—

"Yes, William, they are; you love me now, I see you do; and it makes me love you in return. I think I should always have done so—if—if—"

"If what, my wife?"

"If you had always treated me as you do now, William."

"Then, Elfrida, have you forgotten your love for George?"

Deep blushes spread themselves all over her face and neck, but her eyes still shone frankly through her tears.

"No! William, I cannot deceive you; I have not forgotten it yet, it is so short a time, and it was part of my life."

When she saw the disappointment which gathered in his face, she added, more timidly, "But I have done with it for ever. I would not place myself in the way of it again, for worlds; my great desire is, that he and I should both forget. William, dear, I would not alter my present lot if I could; there is no cherished, treasured love, to stand between my husband and myself; and if you will help me by your own, the day may dawn, perhaps, when I shall have forgotten that there ever has been."

"And, in the meanwhile, will you be happy, Elfrida?"

"I will be contented," she answered quietly. "Oh, dear William, don't be angry—don't be sorry for what is past! If I had not loved George, as I did, our hearts might never have been drawn together as they are now. My trouble and yours, have been all for the best. Everything is, that Heaven ordains!"

"Erida, dear," said her husband, as he embraced her, "let us try to begin life afresh from this day, and when we feel inclined to find fault with one another, remember our own short-comings. I have no right, my child, to condemn you for want of faith; my own married life will not bear inspection. But we will ignore the fact that we ever met, before we met in the hostelry at Chamouni; we will make this our true wedding day— do you agree, Frida?" She nestled up closely to him as she whispered— "Yes! dear William, to everything. From this hour, let us try never to forget again, that we are husband and wife."

CHARTER XV.

VALE.

The events of which I have written here, did not happen so very long ago. The principal actors in the scenes I have endeavoured to describe are still living, and still young.

Ten summers only, have passed since Helene du Broissart was found upon the sands at Chelton-Marsh, and eight, since she was untimely laid in the vault at Ariscedwyn. It has been a sad episode in the history of the Treherne family; but of such episodes few families can boast themselves entirely free. It is well if the generality of such leave no more fatal results behind them than this one has done.

Douglas Cameron, true to his word, arrived in England, time enough to join the family party at the Hermitage on the Christmas-day which followed the return of William Treherne and his wife, from the Continent. It was a quiet Christmas that they passed together, saddened as it was, by the events of the preceding twelvemonth; but one to which Elfrida has often since looked back, as the epoch to herself, of a new and happier existence. Grace's marriage followed shortly upon that time, and Agnes Treherne's took place at Milborough, in preference to Ariscedwyn, at her own request, not many weeks afterwards. She would have waited longer than the six months succeeding the death of her brother's wife; but it was his express wish that she should not do so, and her mother would not hear of anything like opposition to what George said, or thought; and so the wedding was celebrated as soon as possible. I forget the exact dates of the two marriages, but there cannot have been much difference between them, for little Mary Cameron, Grace's eldest child, is only two months older than Agnes's boy, George, who, on account of having inherited, through his mother, some slight look of hia absent uncle, is his grandmother's especial favourite over his brothers and sisters. Dr. Salisbury would not permit Douglas Cameron to return to India again. He wanted to know, for what purpose he had toiled for so many years there himself, if it was not to keep his children around him in his old age. And so, by dint of interest, and still greater dint of money, he procured a very fair practice for his son-in-law, near Brackenburn; and the Camerons have always lived at the Hermitage, with their father, since, and will continue to do so, I suppose, unless the old house grows too small to hold them.

At Ariscedwyn itself, perhaps, the years have brought less happiness than they have elsewhere. The estate is well kept up, and admirably looked after by the bailiff, the servants all do their duty, and Mrs. Henry Treherne takes an especial pride in the interior of the house; but the master is still away, and the place is dull and lifeless without its ruling head. But better times are in store, even for Ariscedwyn. An immense amount of papering and painting, has been going on there during the last summer, and Mrs. Treherne's face has worn such beaming smiles lately, and such an assumption of gaiety, that I fancy the prevailing rumour that George Treherne, is confidently expected home next spring, is really true. It is time he came, for he has never seen the shores of his native land since the " Bellepheron" bore him from them. He served in India throughout the Mutiny, was before the siege of Delhi, and afterwards one of the nearly starvedout garrison at Lucknow, and yet came out of all scot-free, and,'as he himself said, "not so much as shaken." When the war was over, the General under whom he served, wanted George to return to England, and lay his claim to the Victoria Cross, and was ready to send in all manner of formidable written affirmations, to prove that Captain Treherne was entitled to the honour; but you have seen what sort of a man he was. He cared nothing for the reward of a medal, and would not even try for it. He carried his reward for valour, and the thorough fulfilment of the hard work he had set himself to do, in his own breast. He would have liked Elfrida to hear of his deeds, but he felt they would lose nothing in his mother's repetition, and he knew that the two were in constant correspondence. After the residents in Her Majesty's British possessions in the East, had been bound over, by means of a few kicks, and a good many halfpence, into keeping the peace, George Treherne bitterly disappointed his mother by turning his steps towards Africa, for the purposes of sport, as he said. There he fell in with one of the Government exploring parties, and followed their caravans half over the country; and when they were all done up, and obliged to return to England, he still went on, on his own account. For the last two years, he has had a house at Cape Town, to which he returns whenever the season is unfavourable for shooting, and spends his intermediate time in setting up, and preserving, the specimens of game which he has secured. Friends, who have seen his menage and visited England in the interim, say it is more like a museum, than a private dwelling-house; but George still goes on steadily adding to his stock, and I have no doubt will charter a whole ship when he comes home, sooner than leave any behind. However, his mother would be thankful to get him back, even if he brought the whole of Africa stuffed with him; and he promises her she shall not be disappointed of her hope this time.

The Crossley Trehernes have returned to the Lawn at Milborough. William took a dislike to the place after the sad events which had occurred there between himself and Elfrida, and expressing his intention of selling it, his mother became a bidder for her old home, thinking it would be as good an investment of her money as any other. And so the family have lived there ever since. None of the daughters are married yet, nor do I think they ever will be.

I have kept the William Trehemes until the last, because they are the two, in whom you are most likely to have become interested. Since their return from the Continent, they have lived partly at Brackenburn, and partly in London; but they generally keep moving about, and are never in one place long; for William Treherne has never quite recovered the effects of that slip on Mont Blanc, and the fever which followed it. He is not positively an invalid, but he is subject to frequent and severe attacks of pain, and is obliged to be very careful about exposing himself to the inclemency of an English winter. At such times, Elfrida has much to bear, and to put up with; but though her husband is often selfish, and ill-humoured, and exacting, he has never ceased to love her, since the second wedding day that they celebrated in the little hostelry of Chamouni; and when a woman is loved, she can endure a great deal.

They have no family. Elfrida has never had another child, and it is far better it should be so. Her husband is not the man to make a good father, and children would probably only prove a source of pain to herself and disunion between them. As it is, they live in peace.

Elfrida's eldest sister, Mary, has been home from India during this period, and left her little family under her sisters' united care, therefore she can have as many children as she likes about her, if she chooses. And Elfrida, although she is unused to them, is always very tender with little children, for the mother's feeling, once awakened in her breast, has never slept again, but still lives, fresh and warm, with which to welcome her dead baby in Heaven.

One evening, not long ago, as William Treherne, after a day of great suffering, lay upon the sofa in his wife's dressing-room, he drew towards him her jewel-box, and commenced to turn over its contents, for lack of better amusement. There were not many trinkets of value there, for Elfrida had gone out very little since her marriage, and had not cared to add to her stock. Such as she possessed, were mostly birthday offerings, that had been made her from time to time. Conspicuous amongst tHe lot, lay the wedding gift of George Treherne, glittering as it did the day he clasped it on her arm. William Treherne did not seem to avoid the sight, or the remembrance. He took the bracelet out of its case, and turned it from side to side in the candle-light, to see the brilliants flash with which it was studded. Then he said— i i" By Jove, Frida, I don't believe I ever saw a bracelet that I liked better, than this one. You should wear it oftener; it's the prettiest thing you've got."

To this remark his wife made no answer, though she was sitting near him at the time working, and heard distinctly what he said. As he continued to r turn over the contents of the trinket-box, he also came upon the emerald ring, which she had been once used to wear upon her finger, night and day. Can I leave them at a more fitting time than this, when they are sitting together, as husband and wife should sit, heart to heart, no secrets between them, and peace both within and without?tain my former assertion, that Elfrida Treherne is happy. Do you ask, again, why?

"Frida," he said, "you used to wear this ring always. Why have you left it off? They're firstrate stones, and there are nothing like emeralds for a white hand. Come here, and let me put it on."

She was obliged to answer now, and she came close to him.

"William, dear," she said in a low voice, as she looked up into his face with her clear honest eyes, "that is the ring your cousin gave me, when he thought he was going to Canada. I used to wear it for his sake, I left it off for yours."

"Why, dearest?" he asked.

"Because," she said, "I thought whilst I wore the token of my first love, that you would never believe that I could feel a second. William, if I had been engaged to be married before I met you, you would have thought very little of it. You would not have said it was impossible I could love again. Try to think of my love for George Treherne, as if it had happened before we met."

"I do, dear wife," he answered. "If I ever think of it now, it is only to regret my own part in that unhappy business. Let me prove it, by putting this ring upon your finger again. When you look at it now, dearest Elfrida, let it remind you, not only that you loved George Treherne, but that your husband knew it, and forgave you freely."

She could not speak to him in return; she sprung into his arms weeping, and he mistook her tears for those of sorrow.

"My Elfrida," he said, "my dear, patient wife, who has so much to bear with, from my wretched temper, tell me that you are not all unhappy—that I have had the power, during the past few years, of making you at least contented, with your earthly lot?"

The pathetic tenderness of the inquiry touched Elfrida. She raised her eyes, glittering with tears, like the diamonds in her bracelet, from his breast, and answered him with kisses.

"Yes, dearest William, I am more than contented, I am happy. I would not change my lot in life, for any other that I know. I would not change my husband, for any other in the world. I do not mind any trouble, I do not fear any pain, since you love me and I am necessary to your comfort and happiness."

The delight which shone in his eyes was her reward, as he folded her fondly in his arms again, and called down every blessing from Heaven upon her head.

Elfrida says she is happy, and she says the truth. Has she then forgotten her love for George Treherne?

No! She has not forgotten it—she never will forget it! His memory is as green in her heart, as the day on which she parted from him; but the bitterness of it has passed away.,

God, whose attribute is Love itself, has not commanded us to cease from loving. He has only said that we must order our affections aright. To live purely, then, we but need to love purely; and Elfrida's present love for George Treherne is essentially pure. She has ceased to regret that sad, and sudden separation. She has even ceased to regret the love which rendered it necessary, because she can trace the hand of Heaven, working for good, throughout every circumstance of that mournful time. She rejoices when she hears of great, and good deeds on his part—of a useful and contented living, and would no more bring him again, under the thraldom of an unhallowed affection, than, had he attained the rest of Heaven, she would wish to recall him thence, to struggle afresh with the miseries of a sinful world.

Her happiness is a true happiness, because it proceeds from doing her duty. Her love for her husband is a true love, arising from gratitude for his trust in her; but the other love was a part of her life, and while she exists it cannot die. And why not? Because the consequences of our actions remain with us, long after the actions themselves are passed away and done with. We may strive to soften their effect upon others, we may strive by a life of purification to make the world forget them, and in time it may do so; but it is not so easy to wipe out the remembrance of them for ourselves. Our hearts are sensitive, our memories are keen, and life is too short for forgetfulness. Our career may be prosperous—it may be one of happiness, such as this world affords; we may even think at times that we have forgotten, or nearly so; but we deceive ourselves. Memory rushes back at a moment when perhaps we least desire or expect it, and the task has to be commenced again. It is useless strife; it is better far to take up our cross patiently, and acknowledge, as Elfrida does, that the consequences of our evil actions remain with us, and must be endured to the end, infusing a dash of bitterness, though they may, into every cup that life holds out to us.

And yet, with this acknowledgment, I

still main

Because she is living a life of patient reliance upon God's will—a life of duty, and therefore a life of peace. She has numberless blessings around her, and she thanks Heaven for them daily; but no such grateful tears fill her eyes, as those which rise and glisten there, when slie reviews the thorny path which she has trod, and acknowledges, with fervent truth, that there has not been a thorn too many in her way, a tear too many in her eyes, since both thorns and tears were necessary, in God's sight, to secure the salvation of two.

Lightning Source UK Ltd.
Milton Keynes UK
UKOW07f1606120816

280459UK00002B/84/P